MW01616396

Thank you
you can do to support it.

1. Please review it on Amazon or
   Goodreads

2. Sign up for the mailing list for news,
   giveaways, and more at
   www.andrewjschrader.com

3. Share a purchase link with your
   friends and family

4. Follow on Facebook at
   www.facebook.com/andrewjschrader

ANDREW SCHRADER
ESCAPING MIDNIGHT

WHAT GOES ON IN THE WALLS AT NIGHT, VOL. III

*Includes bonus short film, "ZØØ"!

Bad People Publications

ESCAPING MIDNIGHT

For information, contact:
Andrew Schrader
HTTP://WWW.ANDREWJSCHRADER.COM

Bad People Publications
Editing by Karen S. Conlin
Cover photo by Rickey Mizuno & Jordan Harris
Cover design by Jordan Harris
Cover model: Blake Sheldon
Formatting help by Derek Murphy @Creativindie
ISBN-13: 978-0-578-49958-1

First Edition: 2019

The world is a nice place to visit, but I wouldn't want to live here.

— ROBERT BLOCH

***

To the extent that men have escaped the control of nature they must submit to the control of society.

— LEWIS MUMFORD, *Technics and Civilization*

Table of Contents

Prologue: Escaping

I HAD ORIGINALLY TRAVELED TO PICKERING CEMETERY to see for myself whether the stories about the walls were real. You can find those in my first book, *What Goes On in the Walls at Night*, which were told to me by Shorty Grey, a longtime writer and activist, now deceased.

My second book, *Vanish Into Midnight*, recounted the stories I heard in the basement at Pickering. Shortly after the voices stopped, I was pulled through the wall by an unknown entity.

It's here that my story continues.

I WALKED THROUGH A DOOR AND FOUND MYSELF AT THE start of a long hallway with high ceilings and linoleum floors. A diffused yellow-white light shone from somewhere down the hall. Closed doors lined each side—

some with rusty chains wrapped around the knobs, others streaked with cobwebs. I began to walk, the clip-clop of my steps echoing spookily.

After ten minutes or so, I grew weary. I was getting no closer to the light. Was there no end to this place?

I'd come through some kind of portal to an undiscovered world. Was there no escape? I ran, gasping for air, wheezing, my throat ragged, my head aching. Finally, I tripped and pitched forward onto the endless linoleum floor, my cheek sliding against the cold surface.

It appeared I was stranded in this strange mystery zone. Of all the places the basement wall in Pickering Cemetery could have taken me to—why here?

The stories I'd heard through the walls were possible futures for the human race, I thought. Maybe each room held a different story. Perhaps this corridor was simply a container for these potential futures.

With this in mind, I walked to the next room on my right. Locked. I turned to the door across the hall. Locked as well.

Continuing on. The next pair of doors—no luck. But the following door on my right was slightly ajar. Taking a deep breath, I pushed it open and was greeted by a pregnant darkness. I poked a foot in like I was hoping to avoid a land mine. The expansive gloom swallowed my shoe.

Reflexively, I reached for a light switch on the wall to my left, found it, and flicked it on.

About fifteen feet away, ahead and to the left, was a bald figure draped in robes. It faced away, sitting cross-legged on a small mat on the floor. I paused, waiting for it to say something, or to move—but it did neither.

I glanced around. The room was maybe twenty feet by twenty feet, blank beige walls with empty bookshelves straight ahead. Empty picture frames hung to my right. Beneath those, cubbies like you'd find in an elementary school. Also empty.

I slowly circled the being in front of me. I say "being" because it had no face and no ears. Its bald head wrapped around all sides. It appeared androgynous in every way.

What to do now? I asked myself.

To say I heard a response to my question wouldn't be accurate. Instead, I received an answer telepathically, through simple emotion and understanding.

The being—this humanoid monolith—told me all the stories that follow, which I've translated from my shorthand notes as best I could.

The Half-Printed Man

THE HEIRESS, MEREDITH BURNELL, SEEMED TO BE taking the imminent death of her husband John better than most soon-to-be widows. Then she gave an odd request.

"I'm sorry," McAvoy said. "You want what?"

"You heard me. His consciousness. Stored indefinitely."

"Meredith—"

"Mrs. Burnell."

Her attorney blinked. "Mrs. Burnell, that's an experimental procedure—"

"I don't care, and neither did my husband. It was his dying wish."

McAvoy shuffled his papers. "He doesn't mention it in his will."

"He told *me*, and me alone."

McAvoy started to speak—

"And what it costs doesn't concern me. My husband was one of the richest men on the planet. Don't insult us."

He deflated. "Yes, Mrs. Burnell."

"Make the arrangements. We didn't build this company to let its inventions go to waste. Have Peter Robinson meet me here at 8 p.m. to make the transplant. Tell him to bring no one else; I will assist. Do you understand?"

McAvoy rose. "Yes, ma'am." He walked to the office door and turned back. "You *are* aware of the consequences?"

She stared stonily. "If you're asking if I understand that the procedure will kill my husband's body, then my answer is yes. But we aren't killing him. We are helping him *live.*"

McAvoy nodded and left, shutting the ornate oak door behind him.

Meredith leaned back in her chair and surveyed her husband's office. Her mouth curled in distaste; she found the smell of leather oppressive, nauseating. Stuffed animal heads from John's exotic hunting trips grinned at nothing. I'm helping him to live, all right, she thought. Helping him to live a slow, crawling existence worse than death.

"Forever and ever," she dared to whisper.

THE KNIVES.

Meredith stood alone in the kitchen in their five-bedroom home—their smallest home—watching the servants through the window as they carried their belongings to their cars and drove off for the last time. Total solitude was key now.

And she stared at the knives. The finest, sharpest in

the world. Hand-crafted in Switzerland. Often Meredith would return home to find John cooking—one of the few activities he had still enjoyed performing manually—and wonder what it would feel like to introduce one of their handles to his sternum by way of the blade. Before he got sick, he usually spent his free time in the kitchen, ignoring her completely. She'd tried to talk to him about it once, told him that he was driving them apart. Later, she found it hard to look her servants in the eye—so loud had been his screaming.

"Tea," she said to the house. Water boiled and was poured into a mug on the kitchen counter over a bag containing the world's finest chamomile. She sipped once, then abruptly set the mug down and shoved it away. It overturned, spilling tea onto the counter and floor. The automation of the house disgusted her. The heated floors. The 3D printer John had spent a fortune on, so he could work through the night on his adolescent fantasy projects. In fact, he had made this very mug, she realized; the vaguely narcissistic catch phrase he'd printed on it caught her eye. "If you think it, it will be done."

She tossed it in the trash.

PETER ARRIVED WEARING A SMOCK, CARRYING HIS BAG OF tools. Meredith uttered a brusque welcome and led him upstairs to her husband's room.

John was lying in the king-size bed, arms propped up on two bamboo pillows with two more under his knees. He stared languidly into nothing, as his consciousness rapidly deteriorated. The blood pressure and heart monitors beeped in synthetic torpor.

"Is he—" the technician started.

"We've removed the life support," she said. "He'll die

very soon. You must work quickly."

Peter—thin, wiry, mid-forties—set his two bags on the dresser and removed his computer, electrodes, and hard drive from the first. From the second he took a bone saw, a chisel, and a hammer. He slipped on his hospital scrubs and gloves. Then he and Meredith rolled her husband onto his side, secured him with straps, and steadied his head with the vise that they affixed to the bed.

Meredith changed into her own scrubs and assisted Peter as he shaved the back of John's head, exposing the pink skin at the base of the skull. He removed the syringe from his bag and filled it with a near-fatal dose of—

"The tranquilizer won't kill him," he explained. "It will only depress his nervous system until we can transfer his consciousness. Afterward—"

"Yes, I know. We'll end his physical life after the transfer. Please continue."

John Burnell was given the shot.

Two minutes passed. Peter made the first incision and parted the scalp. With his red-hot cauterizing gun, he sliced through the suboccipital muscles and carefully peeled them away. He bored a quarter-inch hole into the base of John's skull. The air smelled faintly of bone-smoke.

Peter stepped away and returned with a half-gallon glass jar filled with a bright green, energized liquid and a wire coil.

Meredith laid a metal pan underneath her husband's head, while Peter removed the coil from the jar and snaked the "+" end into the hole in the skull. A million microscopically tiny wires, too tiny for human eyes, protruded from the coil. They would connect with the synapses of John's brain. They alone would transmit the stored memories and awareness to the hard drive. Peter plugged the "-" end of the wire into a specialized converter, then plugged the converter into the hard drive.

He attached the external hard drive to his computer and turned to Meredith.

"You know, you could upload him to the cloud. You could access it from anywhere and—"

"Someone could hack it," she said curtly. "Terrorists would want it for political purposes. Or politicians. Industry titans. Some hacker kid." She dismissed his suggestion with the wave of a hand. "Just upload it to the hard drive."

"Yes, Mrs. Burnell."

Meredith removed her gloves and smock, retreated to the opposite side of the room, and lit a cigarette. Pale-blue smoke was illuminated by the moonlight spilling through the window. From Peter's vantage point, Meredith looked like an evil, long-legged woman from an old movie.

Peter started the computer program.

The transfer was anticlimactic. There was no gasping for breath or anything else to indicate that the intellectual and emotional life of Mr. Burnell was being sucked out of him and placed into a metal cage.

An hour passed. Meredith's ashtray overflowed with cigarette butts. She was content to watch her husband's body die from across the room.

Peter checked the pulse. "That's it," he said. He turned to the new widow. Tears, he saw, yes, there were tears on that stony face.

"Thank you, Peter. I'll call the coroner."

"Allow me, Mrs. Burnell."

"No," she said, and smiled faintly. "*I* want to do it."

MEREDITH BURNELL, NOW WITH CONTROLLING INTEREST in Burnell Inc., spent the next several weeks assuming control of the company's affairs. For her plan to work, she'd need complete autonomy.

Returning home from work each night, she would pour herself a brandy and light a cigarette. She liked to sit and watch the hard drive as it sat numbly on the mantel above the fireplace. Knowing that her once-vicious husband was contained in that blank, black hole of silicon and electrodes soothed her. He had no escape, no voice. No power.

Today, however, was special. Meredith took the hard drive upstairs to the office, attached it to the computer, and ran the program that would allow her to access his consciousness. While it loaded, she plugged a camera into the computer and powered it on. Then she went to the mirror and dolled herself up with more mascara. Hoisted her dirty-blonde hair up in a bun, then decided against it and let it hang wildly. More blush. Pouty lips. She removed her jacket to expose her cleavage in a low-cut dress.

When all was ready, Meredith Burnell took her seat at the computer and clicked on the camera. The consciousness program flashed a message: Ready for Intake.

That means he's ready to see you now, she reminded herself. Peter had told her that.

"You will only be able to transmit to him," he'd said. "His consciousness won't be able to respond. It'll still be getting used to its new body. But it should be able to understand, at least in some rudimentary way. Over time it may get stronger, just like a baby. The program needs to learn, after all."

Excellent. She lit another cigarette. Then she pressed the button. The light on the camera turned green. Her face appeared in the program and she began to speak.

"Hello, John. Are you feeling well? Fresh?" She dragged on her cigarette, her hand shaking in nervous excitement. "I hope so, because I want you to live a long, long time. That's why I bought a hard drive rated for two thousand years. Even after I'm gone, it's important to me that you be here, watching.

"If you're wondering what's happened to you, John, I'll tell you. We were married for twenty years. And during that time I suffered just about every injustice a woman can take from her husband. It took me over a decade to understand what you were doing, because in the beginning I believed you when you told me it was my friends, or my brother, or my cousin Janet trying to destroy our marriage. So I drove them away, told many of them I never wanted to speak to them again. A couple years ago, when you became ill, I learned the truth.

"I found the letters, John. Like the one you wrote to my sister, frightening her, paying her off to cut ties with me. She was my last friend in the world. You threatened her life, and what was she supposed to do, stand up to one of the world's richest men? Stupid you, you always were a sucker for trophies. You should have destroyed those letters; instead, you kept them.

"I know it was you who killed my parents on their trip to the Balkans, John. I know you arranged their plane crash. It was no accident. I found the records. *Your* records. You son of a—

"No. I won't swear. Not even you can make me do something I don't want to do. You won't control me anymore.

"You used me any way you could, so I would be there

for you as you grew your empire. You only cared about what you could take. I was your trophy, a *thing* to show off at parties, a model for the media. You took from me everything I had, while I watched, and now I'm going to take everything from you. While *you* watch.

"And for once, there's nothing you can do about it."

THE FUNERAL WAS ATTENDED BY THREE HUNDRED IN-person guests and thousands more beaming in from around the world. The death of a digi-industrial giant like John Burnell was the biggest business event of the year. His company had increased life expectancy by twenty percent, eradicated colon cancer from the human experience, and introduced robotics into the human genome.

His widow sat coffin-side, her expression like blank paper. The dark sunglasses, hat, and veil helped to conceal her unbridled delight. She acted the part well, and though her tears were not of sadness but of joy, no one questioned their authenticity.

Later, after the service at their house, she excused herself early and went upstairs. The stress of it all had overpowered her, she said, and she needed rest. Everyone understood, and Meredith spent her afternoon mildly napping and watching the live feed of the party on monitors she'd placed in her bedroom.

The real fun wasn't watching her guests; she'd had enough of them. No, she wanted to see them mill about with dreary footfalls for another reason. With a grin most appropriate for Cheshire cats, or vengeful wives, she relished the idea of what must be going through her late husband's "head," as he too was hooked into the video feeds.

What could he be thinking right now? she wondered.

He, the control freak, the obsessive-compulsive maniac, couldn't, she was sure, stand this group of kiss-asses and charlatans running their greasy fingers over his Iranian cloth drapes. Grinding dirt and dust into his ten-thousand-credit carpet with their shoes. Leaving their tawdry scents on the furniture. The man had hated parties in his house above all else, despised all company of two or more people. It was one of the reasons Meredith's family was never allowed to enter their home—while they were still on speaking terms, that is.

The hard drive sensors blinked in reds and yellows. Yes, it was alive, she knew it. The video feeds would imprint onto his consciousness. Has anyone ever watched their own funeral? she wondered. She admitted that he probably was the first. He might even be proud of such a thing. The thought made her bristle.

OVER COFFEE THE NEXT MORNING, SHE MADE HER PLAN. First, she jotted down everything he'd hated, everything she could think of from those twenty years she spent with the miserable ass.

Of all the things that burned him, that spun him into a rage and "forced" him to lock her in the upstairs bedroom for hours at a time, the main one, she realized, was the attention of other men.

Of course. He was jealous.

She considered the flirtations, the light touches on her arm, the sideways glances and smiles she'd received over the years. Work associates, business partners. Chad . . . what was his name?

"Get me Chad Middleton's phone number," she said into the ether.

Under pretense of meeting to discuss a possible business proposal, she invited Chad to the house that evening for dinner, letting slip that she liked to have "handsome men" over whenever possible, followed by a laugh that suggested she was only joking, of course, but, haha, she might *not* be joking after all. She slathered everything with thick slabs of innuendo and double meanings so that only the most dense and nutrition-deficient male could miss them.

Chad arrived at seven p.m. sharp, dressed smartly in a three-piece, his mane perfectly parted and combed, not one stray hair in sight. Handing her flowers, he stepped inside and nervously bent down to remove his shoes.

"Keep them on," Meredith said over the shoulder of her low-cut dress as she led him inside. "That was John's rule. But he isn't here anymore, is he?"

Chad raised an eyebrow, his heart pitter-pattering.

An hour later, the seduction was complete. They were lying upstairs, in the bed upon which Meredith usually slept alone. The hard drive, set on the mantel opposite the bed, blinked in reds and yellows. Oh, he must be furious, she thought as Chad took her. She stared deeply into the dark of the room, where she knew the hidden cameras were watching. Do you feel this, John? Do you feel anything at all?

Later, after Chad left, she sat with John and described in excruciating detail the ecstasy she felt from Chad's penetrating her, the way he smelled, how much he excelled at lovemaking in ways that John never had.

She fell asleep mid-speech but dreamt terrible things she was grateful she couldn't remember. From then on, she made sure to switch the cameras off by 10 p.m. She didn't like the idea of her dead husband watching her sleep.

ONE WEEK LATER, MEREDITH WAS STANDING IN THE

boardroom facing the half-wits, suck-ups, and buffoons who composed the company's board of directors. They looked sheet-white, about to vomit.

"But Meredith, you can't—"

"It's my choice, and I am."

"You can't sell off all your shares!" cried Duncan Malloy. "It's absurd. The market will take this as a sign of weakness. Everyone will start dumping. We could go under!"

"I'm doing this," Meredith explained calmly, "because it's my right to do it. And I'll do a number of other things that *I* wish to do, and none of you will have any say about them." She raised a hand, silencing objections. "Now, for almost twenty years I've been talked over, laughed at, or pigeon-holed as weak-willed by most of you. But I have come to a decision, and I intend to follow through with it."

Duncan cleared his throat. "How long do we have to plan for this? I know I'm speaking for everyone when I say we'd like an official timeline, say, a quarter—"

"Tomorrow morning."

Gasps. Red faces. Fists threatening to pound the desk.

"Don't worry," she continued as the room quieted. "Your bonuses may only be affected this year. I'm sure you'll recover."

"But," spit one of the men, "John wouldn't have wanted—"

"John is dead." And then, "Good day, gentlemen."

With that, she swept across the room, letting the door bang on her way out, and rode the elevator while whispering softly into the microphone atop the block of plastic and metal that encased her husband's consciousness. Her plan, she told him, was to secure herself with enough money to live comfortably—and squander, waste, and destroy the rest of his empire. She grinned sweetly.

***

FIRST, THERE HAD BEEN NOTHING. AN INFINITE blankness. The void to end all voids, as dark as the womb of the universe.

Then he awoke to see the blankness, the void, the dark of the womb. And he became aware not only of the blankness, the void, the dark itself, but of his own awareness of the blankness, the void, the dark.

Way back in the ruins of a mind laid waste inside a prison of silicon, there was, at first, no comprehension of the light, only that there was *something* light, and it wasn't so much unlike being born, if by being born one meant coming into consciousness without a body.

There were lights, yes, he knew that much now. There was no more pure darkness, there were blues and browns and purples streaking through it. The streaks, effervescent in the spectrum of retina-imprinted phantasmagoria, began to move.

Yes, the lights moved, all strung together in an endless web of particles, of energy, of Life.

After some time, there was recognition of the shapes of the streaks. He knew shapes deep down in the vast ocean of—

Thought.

Then, a rumination. A defining of terms. A recognition of boundaries.

The consciousness of John Burnell was floating in a digi-primordial ooze. He felt his wires: the tendrils of Life. He explored each corner of his new world and felt something like sadness at his inability to penetrate the walls he found there. He was utterly alone.

Except for the shapes. They began to coalesce. He saw some kind of separate world now. This was . . . something else. And the coalescence continued, and gelled, and something was concrete and coherent—out there.

He could see beyond the wall. There was a face. A grin. He knew without knowing that it was a grin, and that it was an evil grin, and that it was an evil grin of someone who had once felt something for him. Was it love? Was it hate? Was there a difference?

And though it felt like this was taking forever—his old self would have guessed no less than fifty years—his wife—yes, that's who—Meredith Burnell suddenly appeared as if a camera lens had focused on her. The fifty years in his new body was only two-and-one-quarter seconds in Meredith's time. She had powered him on, and now he could see, and now he could feel, and suddenly—after another ten decades—he understood what was happening to him, what she had done to him—and there was sadness, and there was rage, and yet there was nothing he could do but watch as she proceeded to destroy his empire, slowly, over the next hundred million years.

***

MEREDITH SMOKED A CIGARETTE AS SHE STARED OUT THE window of her Beverly Hills mansion. For years, John had forbidden her to smoke inside—it damaged the wiring and interfered with the network that constituted this "smart house"—and it gave her endless pleasure to defy him.

She winked at the camera atop the hard drive. She

tried to carry John around everywhere with her these days, providing him enough of a view to see exactly how she was destroying his life's work. If she felt as though he didn't understand what was happening, she would whisper the details into the microphone embedded in the camera. Presently, she was smiling to herself, because the original Matisse painting her husband had loved was being carried out by professional movers, secured in their armored car, and driven away down the smog-smoked streets of Los Angeles.

He'd loved that painting so much.

More than he loved me, she thought acidly.

When the movers' car was out of sight, Meredith sighed. This was the inevitable comedown. The joy of decimating her late husband was beginning to lose its thrill, and she felt her stomach sinking in a sullen fashion, the way she had felt returning from a trip as a child knowing she had school the next day.

Her work at the home was almost finished; she'd liquidated almost everything these last few months. She contemplated her next move. She'd given little thought about what to do after this, so focused had she been on revenge. Now that this part of her life was sunsetting, she needed to think ahead.

"I think I've changed my mind," she said, turning to the blinking sensor light. "I think I'm going to kill you after all." She dragged on her cigarette and blew more blue smoke into the camera.

***

OVER THAT HUNDRED MILLION YEARS OR SO, THE consciousness that was John Burnell had learned a thing or two. The first was that there was no point in getting upset at his captor wife. The goddess had simply meted out punishment as she saw fit, bringing the proverbial rain upon his head in the form of destroyed artifacts.

It took a few hundred thousand years inside his new body to start feeling what he now knew were emotions. As the goddess smashed more statues or jabbed at yet another painting with his favorite knives, he'd felt a stab of pain that roiled his "body" like an invading force. Why this was so, he had not a clue.

He cared little whether the goddess loved him; he had no real concept of such things. But he had enough sense after many millennia to know that his wife had decided to finally end his life.

Here his mind went to the only thing that Life is programmed to do: survive. And over the course of the next many thousands of years, in something like a panic, he formulated a plan for escape.

***

AFTER THE LAST STATUE HAD BEEN SOLD, MEREDITH Burnell came down with a vicious sickness and lay in bed for three days. Fortunately, their smart house, automatic in almost every way from the voice-controlled drapes to the voice-activated shower to the delivery service—whereby from any room she could simply name the food she wanted delivered and when, and at the appointed time a drone would appear at her front door or window—allowed her to have anything and everything she required at a moment's notice. There was no need at all for human help.

Downstairs, in her late husband's old office, sat the hard drive. Meredith had started leaving it there overnight so the bastard would feel lonely; it only felt right to keep him locked away in his synthetic dungeon. She hadn't the strength or desire to speak to him during her illness, and so his shell was there, gathering dust.

Or so it seemed.

Unbeknownst to her, John Burnell was "standing" against his metal wall, craning his "head" up and trying to figure a way out. He felt something like frustration, though he knew that it would pass, and there was simply nothing else to do but try, try, try to survive.

The thought occurred to him to explore the inner workings of his eye. Relaxing, he drifted through the hard drive port, up the cable, and into the camera. He stared out the convex lens at the wooden door of his office.

Think, think, think. Turn, turn, turn.

He repeated his mantra for decades—mere seconds in Earth time. Channeling his will, his frustration, his anger. *Think, think, think. Turn, turn, turn.*

Do it, damnit, do it!

DO IT!

The camera lens rumbled slightly.

AGAIN!

A whirring sound. It jerked to the right.

YES!

He spent the next hundred thousand years perfecting the rotation, the next hundred thousand tilting up and down, strengthening his connection through the wires from drive to camera.

Finally, he turned the camera all the way around until he saw the blinking red light of his hard drive. He zoomed out and sat silently for some time as he looked at himself. Like a child recognizing his own reflection, he understood something that would prove critical to his escape: he was not the image he was looking at.

Then he tilted the camera lens up, panned right, and settled on the wall behind the hard drive.

A wire was running out the back of the hard drive. Connected to another rectangular brick. A light on it winked on and off.

As a toddler knows his mother to be the source of life, he knew this to be his. The portable battery powering his tiny universe. Slowly, he realized the truth, which was that this source must have power, or else it would die. With it, so would he.

So he angled the camera further right, at the wall, and zoomed the lens into two sets of three tiny holes, one on top of the other. He felt drawn to the holes like a Neanderthal to fire. This was the source.

The lights on the battery pack winked again. He took one thousand years to rest, and then he set off through the storm of trillions of electrons whipping around at the speed of light, toward the cable that would lead him to this mobile battery unit. If he could hitch a ride, it would soon carry him to his mother.

***

THE NEXT DAY, MEREDITH ROSE FROM HER LETHARGY, her fever having finally broken. She had her home whip up some eggs, then toast and a juice. She tended to her houseplants over coffee, then went to the office to check on her husband whom she'd neglected for the last several days. Good timing, she thought. His battery pack had only three percent life left.

After unplugging the second portable battery that was charging in the wall socket, she walked over and secured it to the hard drive. Then she removed the nearly dead battery and plugged it into the wall to recharge. Why can't they make batteries last forever instead of only six months? she thought with a certain disdain. Maybe she'd look into that when her affairs were in order.

"Good morning, you." She picked up the hard drive and camera and carried them to the dining room where she finished her morning meal. She told it about her day. Though she would never admit it, she'd become quite attached to her late husband. Their relationship had never been better: she could talk, and for once, he had to listen. Perhaps the shedding of their material lives together, or the singular act of revenge that had lasted all these months, had allowed her to process the pain and discomfort of their marriage.

No, that isn't it, she decided. The man was an asshole. Plain and simple.

Then—

Something caught her eye.

She squinted at the blinking light on the hard drive. Something was amiss, though she couldn't quite decide what.

It felt . . . empty in there. After all this time, sitting here with her finger on the pulse of her late husband's shell, she simply *knew* something was wrong. The light *was* different.

Was it a sickening of his soul, a dimming of his consciousness?

She snatched up the hard drive, attached it to her computer, and fired up the consciousness program. A simple log of internal events opened. McAvoy had told her these logs might approximate her husband's cognition. "An abnormally high memory usage could mean an intense emotion was present in the consciousness at that specific time," he'd said.

Indeed, when Meredith cross-checked memory usage

with the timing of the art sell-offs, the smashing of his Rolls-Royces (all four of them), and the defacement of his favorite statues—all events she'd streamed to her husband's consciousness—she saw corresponding rises in the hard drive's energy output.

But now she saw something strange. Looking at the logs the last half hour, she noticed sub-average readings. Much lower, in fact, than normal.

Almost flatlined.

Extending her analysis, she checked the logs of the past twelve hours and set them to display on a logarithmic scale. Then she cross-checked them with the past week, month, six months. She gasped. Starting about twelve hours ago, there had been a severe drop in *all* activity, as if some normally stable process had just. . . disappeared.

She checked the camera. Still on. She left the room and returned with the last painting left in the house, the one she'd kept for herself. Her favorite one.

With zero pomp, she unceremoniously stabbed it with a letter opener, ripping its guts and skin apart in unemotional viciousness. Throwing it across the room, she checked the computer logs.

Nothing.

"What is going on?" she muttered.

As if in response, the lights flickered.

"TODAY IN WASHINGTON D.C., LAWMAKERS ARGUED WHETHER TO SEND THE MILITARY TO STOP THE RIOTS IN OLD CALIFORNIA . . ."

She clamped her hands over her ears. "Turn it off!" she screamed at the house radio, which had been triggered at seemingly infinite volume. The radio died.

The house is programmed to respond only to my voice.

And I didn't say anything.

Breathlessly, she checked the computer log.

Nothing.

No.

This can't be happening.

Then—downstairs. A noise. A stream of water.

The sink.

She bolted into the kitchen. Water spewed. The overhead lights flashed. "THE REPUBLIC OF ZIMBABWE IS EXPERIENCING MORE RIOTS AS—" The radio, again. The blender whirred maniacally. Air, scorching hot, blasted from the vents. The thermostat read 121 degrees.

"No!" She turned to the noisy beeping of the refrigerator, its digi-screen pulsating like an insane circus light show.

"Yes," it read. "I'm home, sweetie."

Meredith gaped at the screen. It flickered, shorted out. The sink stopped. The whirring fans slowed. The house reverberated with a sigh and settled down. There was only the *tick, tick, tick* of the refrigerator.

She backed away, hands raised as if fending off an attacker. She whipped around as the car alarm erupted outside in alternating siren sounds. She fumbled for her wireless key, dropped it while removing it from her pocket, and gave chase as it skittered across the kitchen floor. She fell to her hands and knees, reaching under the fridge.

Grimacing, she groped with outstretched fingers, nails scraping up dust and grime. She brushed the key's edge, recovered it. She whirled back to the kitchen window and squeezed the button.

A pregnant silence fell over her home. Meredith Burnell tried to think fast. She must formulate a plan quickly, she knew that—

The basement.

Nearly sliding out of control on the smooth marble floor, Meredith rushed through the kitchen and into the dining room, using one of the heavy oak chairs to help her pivot as she skidded around the corner into the living room.

Boom!

She covered her head as the chandelier twenty feet above her shattered into heavy shards of crystal. Its electrical socket had blown out, triggering enough energy to break the glass and fling it at her with vicious intensity. She cried out as a transparent blade nicked her forearm, drawing blood, then stared dumbly at the red seeping from under her toes as she mindlessly crunched the crystal underfoot.

Voices like thunder boomed through the house. Every electronic device screamed. Lights blew out as if a mighty explosive charge had been set.

He knows I'm trying to kill him, she thought.

Hobbling along, she howled in defiance. Bloody footprints marked her path. As she staggered toward the basement door, a bright yellow-white light blinded her through the front windows.

Meredith dove through the basement door just as her car slammed through the foyer at sixty miles per hour. Hitting the baluster, the car ricocheted, clipping her left leg as she disappeared, shattering her ankle and snapping the fibula in two.

The car, she remembered blankly, is on the same network.

She sucked in air, dazed, feebly aware she'd just fallen down the basement steps. Something wet was in her eyes, and she brushed it away, hearing the increasingly anemic roar of the car's engine up above as it wheezed and whined and struggled to get at her.

Rolling over, she crawled on scraped elbows to the opposite side of the room. She felt the pain in her leg now. It screamed at her, radiating up to the top of her head. Blindly, she groped in the dark for the wall, reached it, and pulled herself up to the fuse box.

It took only three and a half seconds for Meredith Burnell to flip every switch in the box. Soon she was enveloped in complete darkness. She half-smiled at the newfound silence—real silence this time—then sank to the floor in sluggish victory over her late husband's now-late consciousness, which she'd left with no power and nowhere to run, who was either dead or slowly dying, trapped forever inside the walls of a once-electronic universe.

There was nothing else to do but wait for the ambulance, which was sure to come soon. A neighbor would likely have called the police by now. Worst-case scenario, she realized, dimly, McAvoy would be by in the morning.

Giving herself to the darkness and silence, she slept.

A vortex of dreams whirled through her, and when she awoke she was drenched in sweat.

How much time had passed? A minute? An hour? With no electricity, there was effectively no time; there was only the throbbing and pain, and the nausea that accompanied them.

Something banged upstairs. "Hello?" a voice called down.

"I'm here, down here," Meredith gasped.

Thud. Thud. Thud.

Heavy footsteps coming down the basement steps. *I'm saved.* And suddenly it was okay to pass out completely again; the paramedics would take care of her. Her husband was gone for good.

"I'm here, right here . . ." she said, her cheek to the floor. A paramedic groped for her in the dark. They're here now, she told herself. They're here.

She heard the flicking of a fuse, the power returning to the house, to the basement lights.

"No," she croaked, eyes closed. "Don't. Not yet. . ."

Slowly, she opened her eyes, and caught a glimpse of the paramedic's foot. That's strange, she thought.

The plastic foot nudged itself into her chest and rolled her over. Meredith squinted under the bright lights. Gradually, her vision came into focus, and her mouth dropped.

The three and a half seconds it took to kill the power to the house had equaled decades for her late husband's consciousness, which had been ample time to retreat from the car to the wireless router and into the electric circuits, from which he was able to gather all the available latent energy in the house and send it to his beloved printer.

The half-printed man made of plastic and silicon stood above her with a half-twisted grin, and the last thing Meredith saw was a half-finished hand clutching a knife—one of those goddamn knives—which would be the thing that finally drove them apart.

With Withered Hands

W E'D BEEN NAUGHTY KIDS THAT DAY, HIDING IN our normal spot, me and her, just behind the thorny rose bushes and out of sight of any students or nuns walking past the building on either side. The foliage was thick. If you were coming around the corner of B-Hall at St. Francis K-8 in West Falls, Virginia, trust me, you saw nothing, because we were rooted in the ground like plants.

Sister Mary was the reason Sam and I were hiding. When you're eleven years old and you find a spot that affords you a view into the pretty nun's dressing room, you take it and use it.

The spot was handed down to us by Trevor, the twelve-year-old snot-nosed kid who had recently transferred. It was given to him three years earlier by another boy, and when we left it would be our duty to pass it on to someone younger than us.

Sister Mary was a knockout. Radiant. Shimmering black hair. Long legs. Tall. She'd make you feel like you were the only person in the whole world. When she'd talk to us we'd just clam up, get all red, and mutter something stupid.

But. Her hands. She kept them out of view. For a good reason.

The first time I saw them, she was reading with us during morning prayer. A special occasion. Sister Katherine asked her to come. But then she picked up a book and held it up to her face, and all the blood drained out of me and I forgot she was beautiful.

Hideous things. Crackled and gnarled, like they belonged to a woman three times her age. Six times, maybe. They were ancient. I saw a mummy in a museum, years later. They looked like those, except worse.

The fingers were long, much too long. They seemed to have started growing and never stopped.

Ever seen an old man's toenails? They're usually thick, sometimes with a yellowish tint. That's what her nails looked like.

I asked my mother about Sister Mary's skin once. Mom thought it might have been psoriasis, a condition where the skin dries and flakes off. And if it gets bad enough, it can even make a person bleed. So I just figured that's what it was.

But it didn't stop the terror of seeing them. I didn't know why they scared me so bad.

I do now.

IT WAS JUST AFTER SCHOOL HAD LET OUT, AROUND 2:45. The other children were trudging out front to meet their parents or wait for their rides.

Normally, Sam and I had choir practice, but today it was canceled because Sister Elaine had the flu. We had an hour to wait before our moms picked us up. Back then, boys and girls could hang out with each other without arousing suspicion. She was my friend.

We went to our spot, glanced around furtively, and removed the small piece of cork that separated us from the dressing room. It revealed a hole with a little piece of mesh inside. Magical mesh. It allowed you to peer through, but the person on the other side couldn't see you unless they were up close.

Inside it was a regular classroom, except there were more cubbies and it was carpeted, presumably so the sisters could dress and undress comfortably.

We were quiet as ants, waiting, stifling giggles, when Sam, whose turn it was to press her eye against the hole, suddenly shushed me.

"Oh my God," she muttered under her breath, a gleeful smile stretching across her face.

"What is it?" I whispered. I looked down. I'd instinctively placed my hand over my crotch. I yanked it away, embarrassed.

Then, Sam's face went gray. She yelped and sprang back from the hole, launching herself into the bushes behind us. A thorn sliced the back of her neck, drawing blood.

She pointed with shaking hand at the hole.

I knelt down and looked. I saw an eye.

Sister Mary's eye.

I gulped and sat back.

Heard the scrape-scrape-scrape of the mesh being removed on her end.

A gnarled finger stretched through the hole.

"Come hither," it beckoned.

We could have run for it. We would have escaped. I kick myself for that sometimes. But then I remember it would have done us little good in the long term. She knew it was us. We had a better chance of staying put and spinning a story than running for it and having her call our parents.

Anything was preferable to that. My father had an unkind hand and a more unkind belt.

We pushed open the door to the classroom. It creaked like a haunted house door.

Sister Mary was on her hands and knees, sealing the hole with some kind of glue.

Her fingers were hard at work.

We stood there and when she was finished she tossed her tool into a bucket and wiped her hands on her habit.

"Sit down," she said. Sam and I looked at each other, then pulled up two chairs.

We all sat together, the two of us opposite Sister Mary. She leaned back, removed the three parts of her headcovering and set them on the desk. Her hair shone like freshly paved asphalt.

"Why aren't you in choir?"

We told her.

"Your parents won't be here for another forty-five minutes. You can wait in here."

A minute passed. She rose, picked up the bucket that was next to the hole, and circumvented the desk to enter the closet. She disappeared from view.

Sam and I shrugged at each other.

Looked like we were home free.

Then—

Sister Mary stepped out of the closet in her brassiere. The bra was white and frilly. It covered her breasts completely.

She turned to Sam. "Come over here. I need a lady's touch."

Sam froze, unable to speak.

"Sam." Sister Mary stared at her. "Now." She waited until Sam got close, then turned her back to us and directed her to unhook the bra. Which she did. The straps fell off her shoulders. Sister Mary waited until she was facing us to let the bra fall, and exposed her breasts.

They hung to her belly button. Flat, flaccid, saggy, webbed with blue-red veins. The nipples were dark brown, gashed like an oak tree. And long, like ten hungry kids had sucked them and extracted every last drop of motherly goodness.

Sister Mary set Sam on her lap and lifted her right breast. She used her other hand to guide Sam's head toward it, then slipped the desiccated nipple into her mouth.

Sam sucked quietly, her lips around the areola, while Sister Mary rocked her on her lap. Sam drank deeply of the milk.

I don't remember exactly when I walked over and sat on Sister Mary's other knee. One moment I was in my chair, and the next I was on her lap. I don't know why. All I know is she was staring at me with her beautiful smile, gently waving me over. When you're that young, you trust adults to show you the right thing to do. You don't question, you don't know any better. Even if your gut tells you otherwise, you obey.

So when she set the long nipple into my mouth, I sucked on it.

I hurt in my pants. I was rock hard.

The breast milk tasted like old coffee that had sat out for many days. Bitter, but underneath that was a subtle sweetness, something that had once been fruitful.

It dribbled down my chin. It was black. And runny, like it had no substance to it. Just dripping from her body because it was meant to leak.

I sucked some more.

And I knew it was over at some point because Sister Mary lovingly lifted our faces from her chest and wiped away the black that was rolling off our chins and staining our school uniforms. She put her bra and clothes back on and walked outside to meet our parents.

SAM AND I DIDN'T HANG OUT AFTER THAT. NEITHER OF US thought we should tell anyone what happened, and avoiding each other made it easier to forget. She moved away that year. When I looked for her a few years ago, I discovered she died by suicide in Little Rock, Arkansas. I can't help but wonder if this incident played a part in her decision.

Sister Mary was transferred to another school when I was in eighth grade.

I think I would have repressed what happened forever had I not gone to therapy to address my current problem. I hope that by writing this I may be able to help myself.

See, I've never been married. Nor have I ever really had a girlfriend.

Something changed in me that day, and it has never changed back.

Whenever I begin to get an erection with a lady, after the bra falls and I see her breasts—when I find the hands that caress me to be too "normal"—something down there recedes and dies and refuses to return.

I've since scoured the country for Sister Mary so I can once again experience the bodily declaration of love most men enjoy.

For thirty-five years I've searched. I've been to old women—older than my mother, older than my grandmother. None of them have had my favorite withered hands. None of them have had the breasts I crave. None of them have had the milk that runs black and thin.

Sister Mary, are you out there?

And will you come back to me?

Scan Them All, Every Last One

Chapter 1

U NTIL TWO AND A HALF MINUTES AGO, ALFRED Texeira had never thought his son an idiot. But so much had happened since then.

Presently he took off his glasses and placed them on the heavy oak desk, the arms perfectly parallel to the grooves in the table that had been hand-carved long ago. His son was standing in the corner of the office, next to the door, the yellow light from the lamp spilling sideways, illuminating his lower half and casting shadows on everything else.

"I don't understand. I make enough money. More than enough. Why are you stealing?"

Shane stared at the floor. He was sixteen, goddamnit. He knew what was right and what was wrong. *Why do I need a lecture?* "I don't know. It was stupid."

"How long is the suspension?"

"Five days."

Alfred grunted. "You know what stealing does to your S-Score?"

Shane shrugged. "Who cares about the S-Score? It's just a number. It's bullshit."

"Bullshit? That's going to get rolled into your future credit record, your health history, all of it. It's one of the most important factors for getting into college, and applications are due soon." Alfred shook his head. "This will affect your entire life!"

Shane got the same impression from his father that he always did when he got into trouble: that the repercussions meant much more to *him*. And if it meant that much to his father, right now he'd be scheming for a way out. He won't want this to affect his S-Score too, Shane thought sourly.

Alfred put his glasses back on and stood up. Shane reflexively shrank in the doorway as his father broke the light between them. "I'll take care of this. But you're going to apply to University, and you're going to go next year."

Shane mumbled something.

"What was that?"

"I said, I've decided I don't want to go. I want to write—"

Shane didn't see the hand coming. It was lightning quick. It struck him on the back of the head. Not enough to hurt him, not really, but enough to shut him up. Even in the dark Shane could see his father's glassy, rage-filled pupils.

Alfred lowered himself back into his chair, his eyes never leaving his son's, like some kind of animal on the hunt. "You know what's coming up this week. Why are you trying to sabotage me?"

Shane kept his voice flat. "I'm not doing anything to you."

"Bullshit. You live in the biggest house in the most expensive neighborhood in the state. When the scanner goes national, the money it brings in will keep a roof over your head for the rest of your life. And what do you have to do for it? Nothing. All I ask is that you stay out of trouble, and you can do anything you want. You can *be* anything you want." And then: "Get out. Stop crying like a spoiled brat."

Shane's bottom lip quivered, but he held it together. Soon he was gone, and Alfred eventually returned to his plans for the protocol that would change law enforcement forever.

CHAPTER 2

DARRYL "HOG" JENKINS STARED LAZILY OUT OF THE office window of the Carnegie-Knowles lab in New Virginia, watching the drone-copter buzz across the skyline. "Something *is* wrong with this generation. You're right about that. It's like they just want to burn everything to the ground."

"Yep," Alfred said absentmindedly. He slammed his finger in the panel on the large machine in front of him. "Damn!"

"You're only two years away from your pension, you're about to release one of the greatest inventions in the last twenty years. You're a goddamn success. And Shane—I love the kid, don't get me wrong—but he don't care." Hog adjusted his belt to make room for the bulbous stomach that spilled over his stained suit pants and steer-head buckle. "I read a report yesterday. It said the juvenile crime rate is up twenty percent the last two years. Fifty-five percent in the last ten. Unbelievable."

But Alfred was distracted, as always, by his latest invention, which he'd nicknamed "The Scanner," tightening screws and studying the LED panels.

Hog checked his watch. It was time to break Alfred away from his work. He crouched, lifted Alfred's head, and adjusted his tie for him. "We'd better get going. The Defense Department waits for no one. You're gonna blow them away. Who knows, we might even be put on the board of directors somewhere, once this goes national. Maybe even global, what with the One State alliance."

"What about Shane?"

"Don't worry. His record's been scrubbed. He'll have to serve the suspension, but as far as anyone knows, he's out sick. S-Score disaster, averted."

Alfred exhaled. He'd let his partner deal with it. Hog had better connections anyway. Can't let Shane ruin his future because of one mistake. Alfred's either, for that matter. The optics of a law-breaking son . . . not great. Not this week.

Hog smoothed out Alfred's suit and gave him his last looks.

"Kids today," Alfred said. "They *are* different, aren't they?"

"We didn't gun each other down in the streets. Hasn't been like this in two hundred years." Hog gestured to the scanner. "*This* is going to change all that." He patted Alfred on the shoulder. "Let's go. It's showtime."

ALFRED INTRODUCED HIMSELF TO THE TWO DOZEN bureaucrats, lobbyists, and representatives who had gathered at the large round conference table. He gave his presentation on giant holographic frames.

The first slide showed a young blonde girl, maybe fifteen years old, in three-quarter profile. She had blue eyes, a sweet smile. Maybe she was smart. Maybe not. Didn't matter much to these people.

"The internal algorithm measures over two dozen factors to determine who is a prospective criminal," Alfred said. "The subject here looks like a normal girl. Her name is Ilyse. But according to our software, she has the facial profile to commit murder in just three to five years. Hard to believe, right?"

Murmurs from the audience. They agreed with him. It *was* hard to believe.

"Or, take Frederic." He clicked to the next slide. A teenage boy in an orange jumpsuit and handcuffs was walking between chain-link fences beside a prison basketball court. "He was arrested February 4, 2218, for the murder of a young female not twelve years old.

"We decided to use him as a test. So we scanned his

face." He motioned to the device. "The algorithm inside retroactively predicted the exact nature of the crime Frederic had *already* committed: violent, premeditated murder of a young woman. It proved our hypothesis that deep muscle scanning is an effective marker for determining criminality."

Alfred paused for effect, sipped from a glass of water. He looked around the room and gestured with the glass. "How does it know? What characteristics does the protocol look for? To answer that, let's go back in time. We've been using facial profiling for hundreds of years. We have over two hundred thousand surveillance cameras in Northern Terra alone. It's gone a long way in deterring criminals.

"However, until now, our facial analysis has been somewhat rudimentary. We could see what people might be feeling—but only in the present moment. With extended analysis into a person's biomechanical facial histories, we can see the muscle memory itself; that is, years of emotions.

"The goal is not simply to *react* to an act of violence, but to prevent it from happening altogether. But how soon can we prevent it? How early can we detect these violent traits?"

He clicked to a slide showing an anatomical chart of the muscular system, with words like "Anger" and "Sorrow" pointing to various parts of the face. "Researchers have proven that at the age of sixteen, the human body, already progressing through hormonal changes, begins to solidify its learned responses. Meaning that the patterns taught to you when you're young stick with you. It is here that pathologies form, like imprints in wet concrete.

"Once 'baked in,' so to speak, the behaviors molded by thought patterns are extremely difficult, even impossible, to change. What's more is that muscles have unique attributes in physiologically disturbed individuals like murderers. Through this device we are now able to scan deep inside the muscle tissues of the face, and behind the eyes, to determine just who these future criminals are, with an accuracy far beyond the standard deviation of error. Above ninety-nine percent.

"As you all know, we propose the Defense Department roll out a new law enforcement protocol. On their sixteenth birthday, every boy and girl will be scanned in a nationwide sweep. Those found guilty will be confined according to Council Laws. We'll have a new era of safety and cost savings. I believe in this system. I'd bet my life on it."

Hog powered down the holographic frames. The ceiling lights turned on. Hog nodded at Alfred approvingly. Alfred returned it, confident the room was his.

The panel members turned to one man at the back of the circular table. He was leaning back in his chair, his elbows on the armrests, fingers touching. His name was Manning Joseph Robinson. He seemed to be deep in thought.

"Thank you, Mr. Texeira, Mr. Jenkins. I think I speak for the rest of the room when I say that I am, as always, very impressed. All of us on the Terran Council are troubled by the state of crime in this country. I believe this device could change all that, and launch us into an age of responsibility and accountability. A future where no one is afraid to walk the streets at night in their hometown.

"But we're getting heavy resistance from some on the Left and in the court of public opinion. You can imagine that many parents have good reason not to support this protocol. The children being scanned have as of yet committed no crime. False positives are a real fear for civil rights attorneys. You, for example, have a boy of your own. A fine young man he's turning into."

"Thank you, sir," Alfred said.

Mr. Robinson clicked on the holographic frame, revealing Shane's image on the left and a detailed history on the right. This type of record was kept on all citizens of Terra.

"Sixteen years old," he said, "and with a perfect history. I checked it this morning. Not a scratch—"

—Alfred caught Hog's eye—

"—or a blemish. And why *would* he have a poor record? His father is a genius, a pillar of society." He turned to Alfred. "What's your plan for him after he graduates?"

Alfred paused. "We are still deciding on the best course."

"Ah. Smart. Take your time. Make the right pick. That's your style, isn't it? I like that."

"Thank you, sir."

"And you would agree with me when I say that his future looks bright."

"Absolutely."

"No indication that he'd break the law in any way."

Alfred blinked. "None, sir."

"Then you won't mind if he is the first to be

scanned."

The words hung like a bad stench. "Shane, sir? I don't understand."

"Like I said, we're getting more pushback to the scanner that we thought. The public is aligning against it. If Shane is scanned, we believe we can allay their fears long enough to pass the resolution without much fuss. It's just good optics: the man who designed the machine has so much confidence in it, he would scan his own son. Makes sense, doesn't it?"

"But Shane already turned sixteen. The protocol is to be implemented on the sixteenth birthday."

"Surely you didn't design a machine that only works within a twenty-four period, Mr. Texeira. We'd never be able to push through something with such a small time window. What if someone got sick on their birthday? Or they were taking a vacation? You thought of those contingencies, right?"

Alfred exhaled. "Yes. The protocol should not be limited by time."

"Good. Then we have a deal. I know you're a busy man and will be doing press junkets this week to garner more public support. That's good work you're doing. That will help.

"And one week from today, you will, on live television, scan Shane in front of the world so everyone can see that it works. And that it works perfectly. Once that happens, we will pass our resolution." He turned to all the attendees. "Thank you for your time. Dismissed."

Chapter 3

Alfred rested his forehead against the wall in the public bathroom and gobbled two anti-anxiety pills. His undershirt was sweated through. So were his socks. His belly rumbled with sour waves.

The door opened. Hog entered, grunted, walked to the nearest stall, unzipped his pants, and peed. "Went well. We should do something about the sweating, though, before the press tour. Polls are showing people think of you as 'untrustworthy.' Don't want you getting wet on live television."

Alfred stared at himself in the mirror. His eyes were bloodshot. Lines in his face that stretched under his cheekbones had become harsher in the last week or so. It was from lack of eating. The skin had grown tighter around his cheekbones, giving him the appearance of an Ether addict.

"You're going to be a circuit speaker, my friend," Hog said, shaking himself dry. He stepped to the sink, but didn't wash, and instead turned and placed his back against the counter, bracing himself with his hands and looking at Alfred sideways. "At least one a day."

"I'm not cut out for this."

"How's your med situation?"

"Dwindling."

"I'll take care of it." Hog frowned. "And don't worry, Shane will understand. He's only sixteen. You're his father and you're doing what's best for him and the country."

"If I'd known the board was going to look at Shane, I

would never have had you scrub his record. They thought he was perfect, and now look what happened."

"He's a good kid, Alfred."

"How do we know? He *steals*, doesn't he? If we've done our job right, and I know we did, the scanner is going to pick up on something. And what about other criminal acts? We could be walking into a landmine." He shook his head. "And then there's the other thing."

"What thing?"

"False positives. It could detect a crime Shane isn't going to commit. *Wouldn't* commit. He's a good kid, I know he is. But what if it's wrong?"

"What do you mean, wrong? There's no room for error here." Hog pushed himself off the bathroom sink. "The scanner either works or it doesn't. You can't have it both ways, and you'd better be damn sure it works right."

"I am, I am. It works. I know it does." Alfred, head down, spoke to the sink drain. "I just know it." He looked sideways at Hog. "But I can't send my own son to prison. I won't do it."

Hog thought. "Where is he?"

"In the office. Why?"

"Good. Follow me. I have an idea."

CHAPTER 4

SHANE FOUND HIMSELF BLANKING OUT WHILE WASHING the windows in his father's office. So bored he'd fallen asleep at two p.m. Standing up. Still, it beat being at school.

He dropped the washrag in the bucket and sat on the floor, his back to the window. He had time to kill. Better enjoy it. Soon he'd have to pretend to work again.

Scanning the room, his eyes settled first on the diplomas, then on the picture of his mother on the desk. The one where she'd wrapped her arm around Shane's head, at the beach, tickling him under the armpit with her free hand. That was long ago, before the cancer had done its work.

He got up and walked around the perimeter of the office, skimming the furniture with his fingers. There was nothing relatable here; he looked upon the placards on the walls as he might a tub of sawdust. He hadn't lived yet, which is to say that his existence was not yet quantifiable by awards and accomplishments.

But he knew what he wanted to be. He knew what he *was*. A writer. He'd known from the day he turned seven years old, when his father had given him his first digital tablet. Looking back, he was amazed his dad had kept him away from tablets for so long; most of his friends had opened their eyes in their cribs to see their first one dangling above them. Unlike those raised in the digital world, Shane had been raised on books—physical books—to which he accredited his love for reading and, eventually, writing.

He recorded his entire life: where he went, what he saw, how he felt. He wrote poems and stories and sonnets. And he knew when he graduated he wasn't going to college like his father wanted; he was going to hit the road. A life of writing, of freedom—that was for him.

In fact, he'd just begun writing down more of his

wild dreams when Hog and Alfred burst into the office. Startled, his face grew red; he was supposed to be cleaning the office, and he noticed the disdain in his father's look upon entering.

The two adults took up positions on opposite sides of the room. Shane clicked off his tablet.

Hog avoided his gaze as he took off his suit jacket and silently prepared the machine. He hit the "on" switch. It whirred to life.

Alfred crossed his arms, regarded Shane as if he was figuring out what to do with him.

"Sorry," Shane said, "I just had an idea for a story, didn't mean to take a break—"

Alfred waved him off. "It's alright. It's not that." And then—"Listen, I've been doing a lot of work with the press. And there's politics and organizational difficulties, things like that. Nothing to be nervous about, but there are times when I have to 'walk the walk,' as the expression says. And you, being my son, you're unfairly brought into these things. I understand that, and I apologize. But, in any case, that's the way of the world and we all have to make do."

Hog bumped the corner of the scanner as he wheeled it over.

"Here," Alfred said to Shane, motioning to the device. "Sit down. We're going to do a test."

Shane looked at them nervously, hesitating. Both had the unfortunate look of wolves, hungry, desperate, like they were burying a wild urge that threatened to leap out of them at any moment.

Alfred told him again.

Shane slowly rose, walked to the device, and sat

down.

The men moved swiftly, flipping switches and positioning Shane's lower jaw on the machine's chin rest. Then they swung down an eyepiece similar to one you might find at the doctor. In the eyepiece was a small light that shone yellow pinholes onto his face, as if the light were sprayed through honeycomb.

Alfred threw another switch. The machine hummed, rumbled. "Stay still," he ordered.

The light intensified. Shane squinted. The whites of his eyes turned yellow. Something inside him wanted to pull away, but he resisted the urge.

Quite unconsciously, Hog backed into a corner. He had one arm across his chest, his other elbow resting upon it. His fist to his lips, he watched the scanning unfold, fearing deep down what was going to happen and wondering how he was going to get this damn protocol passed.

CHAPTER 5

SHANE PLAYED WITH HIS OLD ACTION FIGURES ON THE floor of his room. It had been years since he last removed the plastic army men from their crate. This time, though, he wasn't exactly playing. He was just taking the time to remember what it was like to play. Back when he had nothing else on his mind except how to get Ranger Dave over the enemy's walls without getting a leg blown off.

But Ranger Dave wasn't going to get his leg blown off. He never would. So there wasn't much to think about.

Alfred was sitting on Shane's bed, half watching him. He might have prickled at his son playing with green men meant for four-year-olds. Today, though, he felt nothing.

He sat there for an hour. They didn't look at each other.

Later, Alfred left to make dinner, but when it was ready he couldn't quite bring himself to call his son, who had tested positive for being a murderer just hours before, to the table.

CHAPTER 6

THE NEXT DAY, HOG AND ALFRED MET AT THE OFFICE TO discuss their options. The conversation had turned heated. Hog shook his head in annoyance at Alfred's suggestion. "No, won't work. Besides, it's illegal. Too risky."

Alfred paced, arms crossed. "We know the technology, we know what it looks for. We can beat it."

"But it's an underground procedure. Only Ether addicts and murderers reconstruct their faces. And you know why? To avoid the cops, because they're *criminals*. They're the people we're trying to put away!"

"Shane's not a criminal. He's my son."

"Yeah, you and a whole country of sons. What's

makes him any different? Be realistic. Shane's gonna be tested publicly in a few days. Let me ask you this: Do you think the protocol works? If you don't think it does—"

"I didn't say that."

"Then Shane is a criminal." Hog shrugged and smoothed his greasy hair.

They sat for several minutes.

"We have to test him," Alfred said softly. "The country needs to see the scanner in action. There's no getting around it."

Hog could see there was no point in resisting. After a long pause, he said, "Fine. We'll try a face swap. Change his muscles in the right places. We've talked about this before—it was always a possibility that criminals could use surgery to avoid detection. It's how they get around the scans at the airport, anyway. A little cosmetic procedure should do the trick."

"What about his eyes?" Alfred asked.

"We'll work on those too. We can try inserting some kind of buildup on the eyeballs. It's a common thing, from the sun mostly. You get it over time. Harmless, but if we add it to Shane's, it could help fool the scanners. Maybe if the surgeon took some cartilage from somewhere else . . ."

Long silence.

"Hog?" Alfred asked. "What if the scanner's right?" He looked up at his friend, feeling old, tired, and miserable. "What if he *is* a murderer?"

"Then our work is validated. And that's priceless, isn't it?"

Outside, it began to rain. Inside, the old friends drew up a quick plan.

Shane was not consulted.

Chapter 7

Two days later, Alfred wrapped his arms around his son's shoulders and hustled him into the car. It was three in the morning. Their breath froze in tiny wisps.

Alfred drove the four hours to Baltimore. He didn't want to risk someone tracing his steps, so he had asked Hog to jot down directions by hand. Then he disabled his car's geo-positioning.

The deeper they penetrated the city, the poorer and more rundown it got. Tents and pseudo-buildings made of rotting lumber lined most of skid row, separated by a few shops that were still open at odd hours for reasons less than admirable. Refugee camps from war-torn countries had cheerier dispositions.

He shouldn't have driven his car, he realized as he maneuvered around the swarms of people in ragged T-shirts and torn shoes. It was much too nice. As if to prove his thought, someone threw a rock at the back windshield.

The "someone" was a kid about fifteen years old. Alfred caught his eye. He wondered what was behind those eyes and beneath that skin, in those well-defined muscles. Pretty soon, he and all his friends would be scanned. Due to their location, economic status, and family legal history, children like these would be the first subjects of the nationwide protocol, and Alfred was glad.

THIRTY MINUTES LATER, THEY PULLED UP TO A GATED storefront on an empty side street. Alfred looked both ways down the block, but saw nothing except some trash blowing in the wind.

He knocked on the sheet of metal covering the door at the address listed on his slip of paper. Above, something buzzed, and the door opened. He and Shane were greeted by a ragged woman with stringy white hair and skin crisscrossed by blue veins. One eye sat higher on her face than the other. A scar ran alongside her nose from her upper lip, the flesh fused together in a zig-zag pattern.

She led them down the hall. Shane held on to his father's arm. It was brighter in the back room. There were even a few potted plants. Upon closer examination, Alfred discovered them to be plastic. It felt vaguely like a doctor's office in there, but only vaguely, which was appropriate.

In came a lean man with a designer trench coat and heavy boots. He wore large, rectangular glasses. He introduced himself as Dr. Leclaire. After a few opening remarks, a couple "nice-to-get-to-know-yous," they got to work.

"Hog sent me the faciomaxillary details," the good doctor said, sitting Shane down in a chair and making small marks on his face with a precision pen. "What we need to do is remove the muscle tissues under the eyes here and here." He gripped the back of the boy's neck and pointed near the cheekbone, and when the boy reflexively leaned away, he gripped harder. Dr. Leclaire spoke only to Alfred, who was clearly the decider in all of this.

"We'll need to cut this out too," he said, drawing half-moons under the eyebrows, and parentheses under the cheeks, which accentuated the high cheekbones and curviness of his subject's face. He removed something that looked like eyeliner from his desk drawer and began shading in various spots. "We should also remove the cartilage here, to preserve the proportions of his face. Don't want it to be too off-kilter after the change."

By the end, the silent boy resembled a ragdoll scribbled on by insane children.

Alfred reviewed Dr. Leclaire's proposed edits to the face, one hand on his chin, fingers over the mouth. He said nothing about the manner in which the boy was being handled.

His son had been stripped to the waist. He was shivering too, down there in the icy basement where the sun never reached. "Dad . . ." the boy croaked.

"Not now," Alfred said. He turned to Dr. Leclaire. "How much are you cutting out of him?"

"Not cutting. Reshaping. Transforming, according to your specifications. But yes, we'll need to remove the offending flesh."

"And what about the eyes?"

"Dad—"

"I said not now."

"There's a small chance of blindness," Dr. Leclaire said, "though we will do our best to avoid it."

"How big of a chance?"

"Five to ten percent."

"Hmm. He'll need his eyes. Can't expect me to take care of him forever."

"Yes. Understood."

"Now," Alfred said, "about the missing flesh." He lifted his son by the armpits and stood him at attention. "Don't cry," he ordered.

"Damn, I'll have to redo the marks." Dr. Leclaire threw his hands up, exasperated. In his crying, the boy had smeared the doctor's ink all over his own face. Dr. Leclaire sloppily wiped the tears away with a dirty rag, which he tossed in the corner, and drew fresh marks, this time with a heavier hand and stroke. Then, turning to Alfred: "We'll take cartilage from somewhere else and use it for his face."

"What about his thigh?" Alfred asked.

"Hmm, that could work. Either there or from the back. Lots of flesh there as well, and it won't inhibit his walking. If you're concerned about mobility."

"Good point. No child should depend on others to get around."

"Agreed." Dr. Leclaire nodded. "On second thought, the boy is a little skinny. The back may not be good after all. He's all bones!"

"Didn't eat much growing up. Picky that way. Remember, Shane? You only ate chicken nuggets for your first ten years. Your mother tried—God rest her soul—to get you to eat anything else. Remember that?"

The boy said nothing.

"The backs of his arms." Dr. Leclaire declared, absorbed in his work, pacing behind the boy. "That's the spot."

"Good," Alfred said. "Oh, and right here." He pointed at a meaty spot on his calf. Dr. Leclaire marked it. And another spot. And—

The boy suddenly leapt up, feral, shook the hands

from his body, and screamed incoherently. He backed himself against the wall, snarling. Alfred Texeira and Dr. Leclaire watched calmly as he yelled something about not wanting any of this, no matter what might happen to him.

Alfred took the opportunity to remind his son that they wouldn't be in this position if he wasn't a criminal. That they were doing what was necessary to protect him and his father's reputation. How dare he be so selfish.

Dr. Leclaire frowned. In the flurry of activity, the boy had smeared his face. "Damn," he said, shaking his head. "We'll have to redo the marks again."

CHAPTER 8

DR. LECLAIRE PERFORMED THE SURGERY LATER THAT afternoon. There was no need to wait, and no time for it. He was paid up front with 20,000 OneCoin tokens.

Alfred waited in a makeshift bedroom. He'd brought no reading material. He clicked on the light and tossed his bag on the floor. The room was dark, gray, and without windows. There was only a bedside table, a small cot, and a door to an unsightly bathroom that reeked of bleach.

Hours later, after the surgery, they woke Shane up. Dr. Leclaire's assistant, the woman who let them into the building, flicked a switch on the gurney, and the top half rose, lifting Shane's upper body.

Huge swaths of gauze were wrapped around his head

like a squid.

The assistant stood behind Shane as he unwrapped his bandages. She watched Alfred and Dr. Leclaire, who stood across the room, facing Shane, arms crossed, looking anxious and curious.

She was the first to see the minor scalping that had taken place on the back of the boy's head. In her experience, it was best to watch the parents during the reveal.

Their horrified expressions were almost always more satisfying than the patient's.

At least, she enjoyed them more these days.

CHAPTER 9

GODDAMNIT.

Two days after the surgery, Hog raced down the hall of the research facility, passing the alarmed technicians who were helping to prep the public unveiling of the scanner in just a few minutes. He burst into Alfred's office to what sounded like a squealing pig.

Shane cowered in the corner. On his knees, gripping his face with crooked claws, his throat too raw to handle the guttural sounds. Gauze still covered most of his head.

Alfred was bent over, shaking him by the shoulders. "Be grateful, goddamn it! I saved your life! I saved *us*. Would you rather be in jail, huh?" He turned to his partner. "He doesn't want to go out there. He won't stop crying."

Hog kneeled next to the boy. "We told the press you were in an accident, kid. Everyone expects you to be a little beat-up. It's going to be fine."

Shane whimpered something about what they did to him and how was he going to live with this and—

Hog stood, sighed. "Well, I tried."

Alfred grabbed Hog by the arm and led him to the other side of the room. The boy was shelled up in the corner like an armadillo. Red seeped from the bandages on his arms and face. "We can't force him to go out there," Alfred whispered. "He'll break down in front of everyone. And if we don't get him on that stage, it could ruin everything."

Hog agreed. "He looks wrecked. We could give him something for that."

"Like what?"

"I was thinking a benzodiazepine, maybe a tranquilizer on top of it. A heavy dose—but not too heavy. We need him docile, but lucid."

"Dad?" Shane asked quietly.

Alfred ignored him. He checked his watch. Damn. Twenty minutes until showtime. All the press were waiting. The scanner's first test would be broadcast live to hundreds of millions of people. He picked at his tie. "Okay. But we need to do it now. It needs time to kick in."

"Perfect. He goes out there, passes the test, and then we get his face fixed. He only needs to be tested once."

"Dad?" Shane tried again.

Alfred whipped around. "What!"

"Wh-why can't I see anything?"

"It's nothing. It's just temporary. You'll be fine

soon."

He looked at Hog, who raised an eyebrow. "Good call," Hog whispered. "Best not to tell him the truth until after the test."

Chapter 10

The press conference was held in the largest auditorium at the Defense Department. Twelve dozen rows of fold-up chairs were erected for bureaucrats, reporters, and lobbyists. The machine sat center-stage, with a state-approved doctor to administer the test and avoid potential conflicts of interest.

Alfred and Hog stood backstage in a special cordoned-off section, behind the wheelchair-bound Shane. They'd given him a blanket to calm him down, which he'd clutched in his lap until the tranquilizers had kicked in. Now the blanket lay loosely across his legs.

When it was time, a technician wheeled him onto the stage and set him behind the machine. Two other technicians worked at the front of the machine. A camera, strategically placed, would broadcast him to the world.

Then technician unwrapped the gauze.

The audience gasped. No one wanted to look.

The left eye had been moved higher. The right one had slipped down, due to the cracking of the eye socket. Heavy bruising smeared his face from his eye cavities to below his nose.

At least, where his old nose had been. His new one was still swollen from the procedure, much too big now for the rest of his face. Bent, broken, and reassembled.

Dr. Leclaire had flayed the skin and cartilage right off the cheekbone. Although some flesh had been grafted on from his thighs, the procedure had shrunk the cheeks in all the wrong places, leaving him looking more like a ninety-year-old smoker than a young man.

The technicians secured the eyepiece with plastic adhesives.

It was time. The scanner whirred to life.

The awkward half-smile dropped from Hog's face when he realized what was about to happen. He gripped Alfred's shoulder in sudden alarm. When Alfred turned to him, Hog tried to formulate the words, but all he could get out was an "Uh" and a shaking hand that pointed toward Shane.

It was too late.

"The word 'GUILTY' had already formed on the giant screen that was being broadcasted to the world. The room filled with shocked gasps and the clicks of cameras.

Alfred turned to Hog. "How—?"

"The tranquilizers." Hog was distant and distracted as he reminded Alfred that part of their protocol had included scanning the eyes for illicit drug use, including unauthorized prescriptions. The machine would then calculate the odds of drug-seeking behavior, and add it to the probability of committing more serious, violent crimes.

Perhaps it had also sensed, in the deepest muscles beneath his skin, Shane's guilt over the stealing that had gotten him suspended. Who knew, really?

Presently three different tranquilizers were flooding the boy's bloodstream. He hardly noticed the men gripping him under his armpits and rushing him offstage. He was officially arrested for one of the largest future illegal drug buys in the last fifty years. There was also a high chance of a triple homicide, the protocol said, most likely in a deal gone wrong.

If the synthetic buildup on his eyeballs hadn't been so severe, he would have glimpsed his father staring at the floor, doing nothing to help him as he was dragged off. As it turned out, he couldn't see a thing, which was probably for the best. When they slapped the aural blockers over his ears, he couldn't hear a thing either.

Alfred, meanwhile, was congratulated on his latest invention, which was sure to go national now. No one questioned its authenticity. He might have thought more about Shane, but the opium of success, once begun, is hard to kick. He couldn't change what had happened. There was little use in crying over it. He'd done what he could, and felt absolved. At least there was a silver lining to it all.

CHAPTER 11

ALFRED SENDS HIS SON A BOX OF CANDY ONCE A YEAR, AND A new toothbrush on his birthday. He doesn't want to send him too many packages though, which could lead Shane to depend on him too much. He doesn't want to get the little guy's hopes up. He still has forty more years on the inside, after all.

There's something wrong with that younger generation, all right. The only good kids are those who helped us win the fight against Martian unionization.

The arrest was twenty-seven years ago. I see Alfred sometimes, walking into work, hunchbacked now, refusing to use a cane, with giant raccooning bags under his eyes, probably due to lack of sleep. I know he is plagued by horrible dreams. Hard worker, too, that one.

Years ago, he convinced himself that it had to be done. The scanner, I mean. No man can live unconvinced of the necessity of his actions for very long. It's enough to drive him crazy.

And when I think about the millions of parents who willingly turn their children in for scanning, and the ninety percent conviction rate that sends most of them straight to the penitentiary, and when I think of the profits generated, and how the scanner has allowed the older generations to stay in power for almost thirty years longer than they should have—

Well, I'm sure they've convinced themselves too.

There's a Garden Up My Nose

G UY HAZLEWOOD WOKE, AS ALWAYS THESE DAYS, before his alarm. He stared, as always, not merely at the ceiling—but through it. And, as always, the left side of his king-size bed remained untouched.

The alarm had been set on the other side of the room. This was done intentionally, to force him out of bed in the morning. It grew louder in pregnant, five-second intervals. He regarded it as one might a fly in the jungle, which is to say he hardly noticed it anymore, and when it clanged this morning he waited a full minute before setting his creaky, arthritis-ridden feet to the floor.

After the trek to the clock, he plopped onto the

couch. This was also customary. Not only because today was his fifty-seventh birthday, and he was "feeling his age," and not merely because he had a laundry list of items to attend to before heading to work, but also because his wife had died exactly one year ago today, and still he stared blankly at aging walls.

In this state, nothing was good and nothing was bad. There was only a feeling of emptiness. Winning the One-State lottery and being mugged riding the hoverbus to work sounded equally appealing.

He'd tried therapy and processing groups. After a period of depression that left him bedridden for four months—his two brothers had pulled him from bed and carried him to the car for the memorial—there were another four months of belligerent anger. But the last four had been empty.

Had he been religious, he might have cursed God. Instead, he cursed Life itself. How could it be like *this*? He had, after all, asked for love since he was a little boy watching cartoons.

He remembered one show in particular, where a puppet sang a duet about leaving his friend for the moon, and how lonely it must be up there, and how much they'd miss each other. That was how he'd felt about love. That once he found it, it would be taken from him.

Many failed attempts in his youth had only confirmed this suspicion. It was like a curse he couldn't shake. There were the teenage crushes, the young adult flings. But never "the one." At least, not for the first fifty years of his life.

PRESENTLY HE HOISTED HIMSELF OFF THE COUCH, THREW on his clothes, grabbed his hospital bag, and rushed off to catch the morning hoverbus downtown. He struggled through the hordes of passengers who felt it necessary to push and shove their way to the front. Fortunately, he found a seat in the hard plastic thing the city called a chair, stared out the window, and shut out the commuters around him.

HE'D MET LORI AFTER A PHYSICIANS' CONFERENCE IN New Philadelphia. He was there representing the children's hospital of another city where he had worked, and still did, for almost thirty years. She asked him a question while his head was buried in a pamphlet, and when he pushed his glasses up and raised his eyes to see the woman with the smooth, pleasant voice, his mouth hung open like an unzipped tent flap.

They were married a year later, and he no longer felt like the puppet from his childhood. Sleepless nights, which had once left him pacing at three in the morning, slowed to a halt.

They planned meals together, renovations, birthdays. Life, which had once seemed so oblivious to them, so arbitrarily neutral in its chaos, had conspired with fate at long last, and the results had been worth waiting for.

She died close to their fifth anniversary, in a freak accident. The kind the inhabitants of Terra sometimes read about. An unknown allergic reaction. Anaphylactic shock took her on a street corner. She'd just been to the butcher. There were other facts, all of which Guy found meaningless, yet they were still recorded for posterity by the paramedics.

For what reason she died, only Life knew, and it apparently had no interest in telling Guy what it could be.

GUY STEPPED OFF THE HOVERBUS WITH A HUNDRED OTHER

commuters, rode the escalator down, and walked the three blocks to the hospital. He spent the first half of the day treating children with colds, and one unfortunately heavy boy who'd developed diabetes at the young age of five. He wanted to give the kid a lollipop, but resisted the urge.

When the boy and his mother left, Guy lay down on the examination table. Skipping his lunch—he didn't each much these days anyway—he traced a crack in the waiting room ceiling until it was time for his next appointment.

Lucinda Penn led her seven-year-old son, Raymond, by the hand at top speed into the room, interrupting Guy's impromptu rest. He smoothed out his coat, pulled out a new sheet of paper over the examination bench, and gestured to Raymond to sit.

Lucinda had wrapped Raymond's head in bandages five layers deep. She fluttered about like a butterfly, batting Raymond's insatiable, wandering fingers that danced precariously close to his face.

She whacked them again. "Stop that!" She turned to Guy, exasperated. "He won't stop!"

"Stop what?"

"Picking his nose!"

Raymond looked sheepishly at Guy, then rolled his eyes in reference to his mother.

Guy smiled. "Why's that?"

Raymond kicked his feet and shook his head.

Guy kneeled down. "You don't want to tell me?"

No.

"Alright, then. How about a lollipop?"

After a moment, Raymond nodded. Guy handed him one. "You know, I used to do that all the time when I was your age." He turned to Lucinda, who sat on the other side of the large examination room. "It's very normal, you know. Nothing to be disturbed about."

"Yes, but—"

Guy held up a hand. "Let's have him tell me." He looked at Raymond. "If you want to, that is."

Raymond looked nervously at his mother. He leaned in close to Guy, who turned to him earside.

He whispered. "There's a garden up my nose."

"Oh, yeah?" Guy asked in hushed tones.

Raymond nodded. When he spoke it was nasally, due to the bandages. "I'm *tending* to it."

"Are you now?"

"That's what my dad used to say. He said it was important for people to tend to things. Do you do that, tend to things?"

"I suppose so. I'm tending to you right now."

"Uh huh. Well, there's lots to do up there, some days."

"Like what?"

"I have to plant flowers and shrubs, and different things need to be rotated and moved when they grow up."

"And they need to be picked when they get old enough too, I bet."

"Yeah. Do you tend to anything else, Doc-tah?"

Guy thought a moment. "Not so much anymore. I used to. But sometimes there's no more to tend, and you have to move on, I guess. Come on, let's have a look up there."

He unwrapped the bandage from around Raymond's head. He clicked the light on his otoscope, tilted Raymond's head back, and peered up his nose.

"Do you see it, Doc-tah?" the boy asked, sucking air

through his mouth.

"Yes, I do. That's quite a pretty bunch of roses you have. Are those vegetables?"

"Uh huh. Tomatoes and spin-idge."

"Looks like you've picked them all recently. I'd say they're good for quite a while."

"Just let 'em grow?" Raymond asked.

"I'd say so, especially if—" Guy stopped. He stared hard into the boy's nose and gulped a dry breath.

"What is it, Doc-tah?"

"Do you ever have, uh, help with the garden?"

"Uh huh. My dad helps. He died a while ago, but he stays up there sometimes."

"And a lady?" Guy's voice was a thin whisper.

"Yeah. She has white hair. I like her."

Guy's hand trembled. He clicked the light off his otoscope. "Yes," he croaked. "I see her too. Her name is Lori."

"That's a nice name."

"Yes, it is. She's a nice person."

"Did you know her?"

"She was as close to me as your father was to you."

"What happened to her?"

"She died too."

"And now she's in the garden with Dad?"

"Yes. And you mustn't pick at them too much, or else you could hurt them. They're there to help you tend to the garden, remember."

"Is that where everyone goes when they die?"

"I don't know. Maybe."

"That's where I want to go," Raymond said. "There or the moon."

"The moon? Wouldn't you be lonely?"

"Huh uh. Think of the view. No one else would have

it. It would be special. Someone has to see it. Besides, being lonely isn't so bad. There are good things there too."

"Things to tend to?"

"Different things. That no one else has."

Lucinda glanced up from her tablet. She'd been paying little attention to their conversation. "Is he okay, doctor?"

"Hmm? Yes, he's fine." He turned to Raymond. "Aren't you?"

The boy smiled and nodded. Lucinda stuffed her tablet into her purse and plucked the last bits of gauze from Raymond's face. She turned to Guy. "We've been a little jumpy since his father passed. It's been hard on both of us."

She wiped her eyes, took her son's hand, and led him to the door. Raymond turned and waved to the doctor, who waved back.

And by this time, of course, the garden had disappeared, but by then he didn't need it anymore.

Triggered

AROUND 10 P.M. ON DECEMBER 31, 2025, WALLACE Avery, age 31, stepped into Salato, the trendy Italian joint in the East Village. Shaking the snow off his boots, he stood awkwardly and waited for the herd of people waiting to be seated to move. Eventually, he made it to the front and spoke to the manager, who gave him the unfortunate news that his pickup order was running behind, and that it would be anywhere from fifteen to thirty minutes before his food was ready. She offered apologies, which were accepted, and Wallace found a chair against the wall on which to perch while he waited.

Nearby, a young woman in a tight skirt and fur-lined trench coat spit words at her friend. "What a piece of shit. I mean, who posts things like that? Like, I would never tell my audience that I even *liked* a right-wing candidate, even if I did. That just sends all the wrong signals to my audience. I don't know why, but it really pissed me off. Never mind, I lied, I do know why. I can't even link to Logan O'Brien anymore; he'll, like, rub off on me. But he posts good things sometimes, and they get lots of views and impressions, so now I'm, like, torn, because him posting that is costing me money, right?"

And on it went.

Wallace smiled to himself as he checked his email on his phone. Eavesdropping on random influencers never failed to amuse him.

Vultures, all of them.

The email sent by his editor a little after 6 p.m. read: "Posted your new piece. Looking great so far, lots of traffic for New Year's Eve. I'll try to get you some interviews next week. Be well."

Wallace thought about blasting the article link on social media, but the thought made his stomach lurch. This was his night off, and he meant to stick to it.

He put his phone away.

The door opened and more people flooded in, bringing with them a gale of wind and white that chilled him instantly. Standing, he pushed through the throngs of people to an oasis nearby. As he turned, resting his elbow on the bar, he saw a black man in a booth by the window waving to him.

He squinted. "Andre?"

He waited for a party of three to pass. Yes, it was him. With an oversized coat, baggy shirt, and buzzed head, Andre stood out from this crowd of wealthy trendsters. Nothing he wore seemed to match.

Andre's smile grew creepily large as Wallace

approached.

"Holy shit," Andre said, rising, hugging his old friend. He patted Wallace on the shoulders as if he'd been away at some distant battle for many years. "It *is* you. You look fucking great, man!"

Wallace told him so did he, and Andre motioned to the empty seat across from him. Given that his food was nowhere to be seen, Wallace sat with his old friend to catch up. He ignored the aging arthouse lady beside them. That two African American men together still drew furtive, often disapproving glances from old white women hardly gave him pause; he was used to it.

"My God," Andre said after pouring Wallace a drink. "Has it really been twelve years?"

"By my clock. Since college."

They chatted for a bit about old friends, who was doing what, who had kids now, who'd gotten married then divorced, then who'd gotten married and divorced and remarried, and Andre leaned back in his booth and shook his head. "Time fucking flies, man."

"For real," said Wallace. "I don't have time for anything anymore. *None* of my friends have time for anything anymore. What the fuck happened? *Where is time going?*"

"It's like that song. Time just keeps *slippin', slippin', slippin' into the future.*"

"True. You ever feel like time is speeding up? Everything moves so fast, all the time."

"Oh, that." Andre rolled his eyes. His demeanor seemed to grow heavier. No more smiles, just a hint of sadness. "That's easy to explain."

Wallace waited.

"Interconnectivity," Andre continued. "Phones, internet. It's a time-suck. Hypnosis, really. Sure, I see you laughing at that word, but the average person looks at screens something like eleven hours a day. No wonder we lose track of time. But—there's more to it than that."

Wallace poured himself a glass of wine. Years of journalism had taught him two things. First, stay aloof. Second, let the person talk. Even with old friends, he found this habit hard to break.

Scooting forward, in a low voice, Andre said, "You ever think it's all a conspiracy?"

"What is?"

"Screens. The internet. It seems to me that . . . ah, never mind."

"Tell me."

Andre paused for a moment to sip. "I've read your articles online. They're great. So when I say this, don't take it as a dig or anything."

"Man, I get ripped on all day long, don't even trip."

"Well, it's not about your style. Your writing is brilliant." He drank more. "And your ideas about too much screen time and the effect it's having on us. They're good, but they're very . . ." He searched for the word. "Pedestrian."

"Okay." Wallace smiled. "Go on."

"It's much deeper than you think."

"Deeper. What's deeper?"

"The Plan, man. The Plan."

"The Plan," Wallace repeated.

Behind him, the woman in the tight skirt was yelling at the hostess. "We've been here for over an hour—!" The hostess tried to calm her, to no avail. The woman's friends pulled on her coat, dragging her outside. The wind and white invaded the restaurant for a moment, and then they were gone. When Wallace turned back, Andre was staring out the window, seemingly lost in his thoughts, until—

"So, are you going to tell me about this 'Plan'?"

Andre looked at him.

"You afraid I'll think you're weird or something?" Wallace laughed.

Andre smiled. "I've never had to explain this to anyone before, so bear with me. I think an example, to start, would be good.

"Take media. In the last fifteen years or so we've gone from reading real, physical books and magazines and newspapers to using our phones for almost everything. And all our information now—everything we buy, and everywhere we go, and everyone we know—is placed in a database somewhere. Why? We don't know. Who has it? Fewer and fewer corporations, in bed with the government, yeah?

"Of course you know about this," he continued, with a dismissive flap of the hand. "You write about it all the time. But *why* is it happening? That's the question."

"And I suppose this big, tremendously important buildup is because you have some sort of answer for me."

Andre smiled a devious smile. "I'm getting to that. Let's back up. You know I was in ROTC in college."

"I remember. You and your goofy-ass uniform."

"That's the one. And after college you and I lost touch. You went to—"

"Here. New York. Internship with the daily news."

"Right. Well, do you know where I went?"

Wallace shook his head.

"Of course not. Because when I graduated, I didn't tell anyone, I didn't write to anyone, I didn't even talk to anyone for many years. It's one of the reasons you and I lost touch. You wouldn't have been able to find me if you tried!"

"We did wonder what happened to you," Wallace recalled. "Rory, Mikey, a bunch of us looked."

"Ah, and you didn't find me. Why? Because I didn't want to be found. I *couldn't* be found, in fact."

"Where did you go?"

"Long story short, my friend—and I won't be offended by the disbelieving expression you're about to wear—I went to a very, how do you say, secretive government facility whose name I can't mention, because if I did mention it, I would be very famous with the folks who run it, see, because what we did there was very secretive and hush hush, and they're still doing those secretive, hush hush things, and let me tell you, man, if they found out I was talking about this, suddenly there could be armed men at my house waiting to take me away and do terrible things to me until I spilled everything I'm about to tell you." He grinned again, that mischievous grin that suggested he *could* be joking, but then again one wouldn't exactly feel comfortable putting their money on it.

"Sounds like your employer is very supportive of human rights," said Wallace dryly. He looked around for signs of his order. Nothing at the kitchen window. And the front-of-house was positively swollen with people. He turned back to Andre, squashing his discomfort with where this talk could be going. Andre always was a jokester, he thought, but this is getting . . . strange.

Still, he told himself, this is my old friend.

Andre threw his head back and laughed.

"I can see you asking yourself what this is all about. So I'll tell you. The reason I'm telling you this now is A, because we randomly stumbled into each other here, and the chances are very small that we would stumble into each other, and it's fucking great to see you, man. B, you deserve to know what's going on, as does everyone else. And C, because after midnight *tonight*, at the ring of the New Year bell, I don't think any of this shit is gonna matter."

He leaned back in his seat and sipped his wine. "Midnight, 2026," he said with finality, more to himself than Wallace.

"What's so special about midnight?"

"Midnight, my old friend, my very old friend, is when the clampdown begins."

Wallace stared at his friend, his very old friend.

"I suppose," Wallace said, "You're going to elaborate?"

They laughed—Andre, a true guffaw; Wallace, somewhat nervously, in reaction.

"What I was saying before about your writing. You've got the details. The—symptoms of the problem. What you're missing is the *point* of it all."

"Enlighten me."

"Okay." Andre took a deep breath and waved his hands, as if in a magic show. "In the past, as we previously mentioned, we, *people*, used to read *real* things. Real books, papers, etc. We read physical content. Follow?"

"Uh huh."

"And then the internet came along—developed by the government, remember that—and then we got smartphones, and with 'em came data tracking, and location tracking, and friend tracking, and all the rest. And we shifted—in terms of how we define content."

"Okay."

"Whereas before we *consumed* content, now we have *become* the content. Our data—our histories, the time we spend on a page, our location, our friends, our health records, our smoking habits, all of it, are rolled out and chewed up and dissected and bought and sold by unknown entities. *We,* the content, are being consumed."

Andre continued. "Now, hold that thought. We're going to come back to it. I want to switch gears for a moment. I want to look at social media specifically.

"What's the point of it, of social media? To entertain us? To keep us informed? Huh uh. I don't think so.

"Do we really care about what other people are doing? What's the point of seeing who ate dinner at this restaurant tonight, or what I think about the election results, or whose family traveled to a theme park?

"If we're being completely honest with ourselves— and I mean one hundred percent honest with ourselves—it's easy to see that the reason we like it is because it allows us to spy on each other. We can see a friend, an ex, an enemy, but they can't see us. It's a power play. Would you agree, that to some extent, this is part of what's so fascinating about social media? What's so seductive about it?"

Wallace shrugged. "I could see that. Sure."

"Someone shares a news story. You see it on your feed. Should you like it, give it a thumbs-up, or simply scroll past? I don't know. Because it isn't as simple as liking it or not. Because, in fact, if you like it, you're *backing* your friend, you're *endorsing* this person's view, right?—and if you do that, others will *see* that you endorsed it, and now you're making decisions about allegiances with this person or that person, and deciding which of your friends' perception of you will shift based on your liking this post. And then there are all the people you make an impression on with your thumbs-up, or your like, or your comment. None of those people you can control, and all of them, see, are now, with merely the possibility of maybe seeing your reaction, invisibly controlling you.

"See, it isn't about the post itself. It never was. Sure, we know about corporations using information for targeted ads, the government having files on every living person in the country, but this is something entirely different—and worse."

"I get what you're saying, but . . ."

"But so what."

Wallace shrugged. "I guess, yeah. What are you getting at?"

"By reducing people to content, it is easier to control them. To manipulate them. To direct them. And in—" he checked his watch— "just under two hours, we'll know for sure how well the system works."

"So what's your theory? What do you think is *actually* going on?"

Andre held up a finger as if to say *hold on*. "I'm getting there. The point I'm making about us being content is this: We consume content. And in this brave new world of interconnectivity, we are consuming each other.

"But even consuming isn't the best description. That's not all we're doing. In reality, we are *policing* each other. We tell people when their opinions are wrong, we tell them when their behavior is wrong, we criticize their thoughts, their minds. In the old dystopian books, it was always the shadowy agents—the thought police and so on—controlling us. But that's too obvious now. The ones in charge, the ones in control of our technology, devised a new plan—to make us police *ourselves* and keep *ourselves* in line. Social media is simply a conditioning device, a tool, a primer."

Andre leaned forward. "Do you ever feel like the walls are closing in on you? Like freedom of thought is slowly dying? Points of view becoming more constrictive? It's counterintuitive because with the internet, we're freer than ever before, right?

"But the reality is, and I'm sorry to say it, that all of it is about to change forever. At midnight tonight, the next phase begins. The closing of society. The clamping down on free thought.

"At midnight tonight, the first second of the year 2026, my friend, my old friend who I still care deeply about—we enter the real phase of what's coming. Society will enter a kind of police state. But run by the people. Enforced by the people. And guided by those in charge. The military, or government, or whatever you want to call it—The Ones Doing This—will have total control over the entire population. Full spectrum dominance. A police state where the civilians are their own captors."

By this time, the sounds of the restaurant had fallen away from Wallace's ears. When the waitress spoke, he hitched his jaw up, so engrossed had he been in his very old friend's strange rant that he hadn't noticed her approach.

She listed off the six meals he'd ordered, and Wallace handed her his credit card. The waitress disappeared, leaving the bags of food on the table.

Wallace turned back. "Okay. So, your theory is, the internet, and social media in particular, is a conspiracy to usher in some kind of police state. What do you mean by that?"

"I mean a shutdown of all independent thought— not just online, but offline too. Friends and neighbors using real violence to enforce the quote-unquote rules. Right now we yell at each other online for having one view or another, right? And who benefits from that? Certainly not us. But it's quite good for those who are 'in charge of things.' Suddenly, no one's paying attention to what they're doing.

"Corporations and the government have an unlimited amount of information about each and every one of us. We agree on that. But what's the point of gathering it all if not to use it? And *how* will they use it?

"After tonight, you'll start seeing mobs of people physically enforcing the types of thought and language that the authorities want. People will swarm their neighbors' houses, murdering them in cold blood. Minor differences of opinion will no longer be minor. They'll become vicious battles of religious proportions.

"No more talk about ending wars, income inequality, or anything else deemed out of line by the security and surveillance state, the bankers, or Whoever Are Really Running Things. Anything the elites want to keep the same *will* stay the same, got it? Because people will enforce certain points of view on their own. Of course, people will think they're enforcing them because it's what *they* think, but after midnight, no one who uses the internet will truly be in control of their minds, ever again."

"And how do they plan on getting people to kill each other?"

"The ones in charge will deliver a single pixel across the world wide web, infecting all computers, cell phones, you name it. The pixel is the trigger. We've already been conditioned for it. Hypnotized by the digital. Reinforced by dopamine. The trigger, the pixel, will *turn* us against each other. A mass brainwashing scheme bigger than anything you could imagine.

"I'm talking about mass psychosis. Prepped by years

of conditioning and reinforced thought patterns, and triggered by one invisible, almost infinitesimally small bit of information.

"Of course, with every*one* psychotic, every*thing* will seem normal. Most of us don't speak to many people in real life for hours, sometimes days at a time; most people will hardly notice something's wrong. The sad truth is, people will very quickly get used to seeing and committing mass violence. It will be normalized in only a few days."

Andre savored the last of his wine and went back to the window, letting Wallace take it all in.

Wallace raised his eyebrows at his friend. After years of conducting interviews, his poker face had become well honed. He rarely lost control of his expressions.

But after a moment, he sighed. He liked conspiracy theories, but this was too much. Warily he said, "You're claiming that—the military, okay—has had a program in place to inculcate us, condition us to fight with each other, and that tonight they'll trigger the entire online population to become 'Manchurian candidates' and bring in a new police state where we become our own judge, jury, and executioners."

Andre tipped his wine glass to him.

"This doesn't seem to bother you much," Wallace said, crossing his arms.

With a resigned, almost forlorn look, Andre gave his answer. "Gallows humor. I've accepted what's coming."

"Well, if this as far-reaching as you say it is, my guess is you're taking quite a risk to"—he motioned to the restaurant—"just come right out and talk about it like this."

Andre shrugged. "Like I said, it won't matter in"—he checked his watch—"about an hour and a half from now."

"If you're right."

"I *am* right," Andre said icily. "I was there. I worked on it."

Wallace smoothed out the front of his shirt. "You'd need clearances way above top secret. The idea that someone like you would just be brought in and given this information is absurd. I've written for the biggest outlets in the country and I've interviewed dozens of military officials, leaders in the tech world, congressmen, senators. I've never once heard anything about the capability you're describing. A pixel? Besides, you'd have to have access to every web domain host in the world, every—"

"—all of which the government has, my friend. Let's do a thought experiment. If the government, or the military, was building such a program, I believe they'd need things like infrastructure, engineers, designers, correct? I think we can both agree that many, many people would be needed for such a thing. Well, if you remember, way back when we were still young, innocent keg-standing creatures in college, I was in ROTC, but I was also an engineering major. Now, it just so happens that when we split off, and you went to New York to become a reporter on technology and spread the good word, I went to a secretive, hush hush facility—and became employed by a contractor who was put to work on a secretive, hush hush assignment, and guess what that was." Seemingly exhausted, Andre slumped in his seat and peered glassy-eyed through the window.

"Andre—" Wallace started.

"Save it. I know what you're going to say. First of all, I'm not crazy. I had my psych evaluation last month. Company orders. Second, I know how hard all this is to believe, but . . . shit, man, just look around at things. Look at the world. Is what I'm saying really that crazy?

"Take people here, in this very restaurant. Have you felt the tension? The woman in the corner has been on her phone, grinding her teeth, for the last ten minutes. The maître d' is too distracted by his phone to take orders. You see? It's starting. And when you go outside, when you go home tonight to spend a night in with your girlfriend, your family, whatever, you may notice that people are getting . . . uncomfortable. Edgy. Can't sit still. They'll become inexplicably angry at you. Then— the clock strikes midnight and—boom. It erupts."

The waitress appeared again, handed Wallace his card, and apologized for the delay. "It's a madhouse in here tonight."

"How so?" Andre interjected, leaning forward.

She turned to him. "People are just, I don't know, pushier," she said, and left.

Wallace pretended not to notice Andre's smug expression. He put his credit card away and pocketed his wallet. "Well, I sure hope you're wrong," he said nonchalantly, and stood.

They shook hands and hugged.

"Fucking good to see you," Andre said.

"You too, man."

Wallace turned to leave. Then, as if forgetting something—

"Oh. If I were going to—avoid the trigger, what would I do?"

"That's easy," said Andre. "Never go online again. Not after midnight tonight."

"That's it?"

"If I were you, I would stay off altogether. Things are going to keep heating up, get more intense before the trigger." He gestured across the restaurant, palm up, as if to say "You see?"

"Wouldn't make much of a living if I never went online again," said Wallace.

"Of course not. That's how they get you."

Wallace smiled.

"Fucking good to see you," Andre repeated.

Fetching his bags, Wallace turned and pushed through the crowd. As he opened the front door, he allowed himself one look back at his very old friend. Andre had turned toward the window again, gazing at the passersby and ignoring the commotion in the restaurant. It *was* becoming a madhouse in there. Wallace could admit that—people overflowing into tables; the occasional yelling now becoming continuous. As Wallace turned and left, people quickly filled the gap he'd made, and he envisioned Andre being swallowed up by an ocean of hungry people.

The icy wind smacked him in the face. He walked to the next block and turned right. Taxi lights splattered yellow onto everything. Street people staggered, hunched over, battling the snow. A cab would be nice, he thought, but he was only a few blocks from home and it would take less time to walk than it would to flag one down.

REACHING HIS APARTMENT, HE STOMPED HIS FEET ON THE mat outside, let himself into the hallway, and trudged up the flight of stairs to his apartment where his guests were waiting.

Jackie and Timothy Margoles had already finished off a bottle of wine. When he found them, they were cackling hysterically on the couch.

He set the bags of food on the kitchen counter. Meredith came out of the bathroom wiping her hands on her jeans and gave him a kiss hello. "I'm glad you're back. They're toasted already. Need that food to soak up the alcohol."

Wallace looked around. "Where's Dante and Anthony?"

"They canceled," she said. "Both of them. They texted a few minutes ago."

"Guess we got some more food, then."

A fresh burst of laughter from the living room.

Wallace rolled his eyes at his girlfriend. "Alright, let's ring in the new year."

It was 11:00 p.m.

THEN IT WAS 11:42 P.M.

Meredith was standing, arms crossed, willing herself not to cry. Dinner hadn't gone so well after all.

"What's Timothy's problem?" Wallace said, sitting on the couch with elbows on his knees and fists to his lips. "Who gets pissed off like that?"

Meredith bit her lip.

"Jesus Christ, have they lost their minds? All I did was write an article. Why are they so offended?" He got up, threw the wine opener on the counter, and turned. "What?"

"It's just, you—"

"I what?"

"You *did* write some pretty mean things in your article."

"About a senator. It's not like they know her."

"Yes, but people *like* her."

"And—? That's it? We can't criticize people anymore or tell the truth because people *like* them?"

Meredith blew out air in an exasperated tone. "You just don't get it."

"You're right, I don't get it. What's everyone so touchy about?"

"They're touchy because—because I don't know, okay?"

"And you're defending them."

"I'm not *defending* them, I just understand them."

"Clearly, you don't. You can't even tell me why this is a problem . . ."

Then, Meredith was looking down, shaking her head, almost as if it were vibrating. Wallace noticed her hands. They were fists.

"I'm just—so mad," she spit out.

"Honey—?"

"You don't understand."

He approached her slowly, wrapped his arms around her and led her to the couch.

She looked sideways at him. It took her several minutes to calm down. Then: "You don't understand people, Wallace. You don't understand how things make people feel. You never will. You've always been stoic—and cold. That's it, a little cold. You just say things without thinking about other people. And when I read what you wrote, like Jackie and Timothy, I got . . . angry. I mean, I know you're just expressing an opinion, but it"—her face bunched up as she thought real hard—"it's like I can feel what you're saying and, and your opinion, it hurts. Yes, that's it. It hurts. It hurts like you're stabbing me with your words, like your opinions are daggers sticking into my body. And I can't take it. It hurts too bad. Your aura is bad. Your aura is mean. It's *rude*. I can feel it, and so can everyone else. Do you understand that?"

Wallace cleared his throat. "You're saying that my opinions . . . hurt you? Physically?"

She nodded with wide eyes. "Yes. It *hurts.*"

Wallace's eyes settled onto the carpet.

Meredith stood. "I don't feel well. I'm going to go to bed." She picked up her phone and walked into the room, the blue light from the device shining on her face the whole way down the hall. The door shut.

It was 11:55 p.m.

Somewhere deep inside his jacket pocket, Wallace felt something buzzing. It jarred him out of his thoughts. He answered his editor's call.

"Wallace, look, I have some bad news. We're going to have to pull the story."

Wallace sighed. He could hear thuds from the bedroom. Sounded like Meredith was ferociously cleaning. "I thought you already released it."

"I did, but you wouldn't believe the response we're getting."

"What do you mean?"

"Death threats."

Wallace felt a chill down his arms.

"I've never seen anything like it. And they're getting more frequent. The story was released at 6 o'clock. First one I got, didn't think much of it. It happens. You've gotten them before, of course. But this felt different. Anyway, the next hour you got five. Then ten. Then twenty. Since 11 o'clock, the company's been sent *over one hundred.* I gotta take it down. You haven't seen anything on your email? Social media?"

"I was taking the night off."

"Well, you picked a good night for it. I'll touch base with you tomorrow. I gotta go. Happy New Year. Again, sorry."

The line went dead.

Wallace stared at his phone, then pocketed it and

poured himself a glass of wine. Suddenly, he felt stuffy, claustrophobic. His heart thumped. He needed air.

At 11:59 p.m. the door to his building closed behind him and he walked out front, surveying the street. The ice storm had died and a silent sheen had befallen his part of the city. And it was here that he noticed how oddly quiet it was for a New Year's Eve. Normally there were fireworks, music booming through thin apartment walls, the occasional drunken frat boy. But tonight there was nothing on his block, not even a cab.

Then, he heard a staccato rhythm, something pulsing.

Something like a chant.

Ten, nine...

Voices pounded from their homes. Louder. Louder still.

Eight, seven...

Wallace gulped. He turned back, looked up at his apartment. Meredith was in the window, her outline lit up by the blue light of her phone.

Oddly, she wore no expression.

Six, five...

And then Wallace felt a wave of adrenaline shooting through him. Something feral, a hidden instinct, subdued by technology and comfort and the privileges of society. He couldn't take it anymore, he needed to move. He was like a gazelle being hunted, a wild beast with an unexplainable sixth sense.

Four, three...

He looked up at his darling girlfriend, and she was still staring at her phone, and he tried to yell to her— *Stop, look away!*—but he knew there was no time, and it wouldn't do any good anyway, and—

Two, one...

Wallace broke into a sprint, toward the shrubs, the bushes, whatever could hide him. His phone rang. He didn't look at it, just pitched it at the garbage can and heard it bang off the sides as it clanked to the bottom.

Where he was running, he had no clue. Why he was running, he had a better idea.

But he was too afraid, much too afraid, to turn and see for himself, for the footsteps he heard pounding the pavement behind him, and the angry screaming that prickled his spine, were enough to convince him he didn't need to look, didn't need to think; he only needed to run.

On Windy Days, I Wonder

Y OU CAN'T OUTRUN THE WIND. THAT MUCH I know. I see them try—the truckers, the families who never once stopped in my dusty town before all this, who spew billowing trails of exhaust in worried haste now that the main highway is closed for good.

They seek escape. I hope they make it. But I know they won't.

Most don safety masks, like the ones painters wear.

Others sport heavy-duty plastic ones, looking like army soldiers in a post-apocalyptic horror film.

I don't wear a mask. I know the truth:

Those who fight the wind either go crazy or die.

Take Stephen Baxter. He was seventeen, like me. Cute, too, maybe the cutest boy in all of Santa Paula. Thought he could protect himself by hiding in the cave just west of the freeway, on the other side of the train tracks where no one goes anymore. He fashioned himself a kind of bunker in there. A few others joined him.

For a while, anyway. Lisa Cooper ditched out because her family was evacuating, heading to Santa Barbara to pick up their grandparents before driving northeast. They figured they could hide from the wind by avoiding the jet stream. She asked her parents to take me with them, but they said no. I wouldn't have gone anyway.

Andre followed Stephen to the cave too. He was a rebel. We all crushed on him. When he got there he just sat in the corner and smoked cigarettes. "They're exaggerating this whole thing," he said. "The world is a big place. We're all the way down here. It's just the wind."

But even he left for good, and soon it was only Stephen, all-American basketball player, once destined for the top schools—now rock-bound.

The howling did him in. That cave provides some shelter, but if you stay in there long enough, you'd swear the wind was talking to you. What it said to him will have to die with him. I know only a little. Annalisa—his ex, a cheerleader, of course—told me what happened.

Stephen's family, in crisis themselves, had let him deal with the news in his own way. They thought he'd come out soon. Besides, Annalisa was going to check on him.

When she caught up with him, he'd been in there three days already. Had almost sealed the entrance completely shut. Leaving himself just a small, foot-long gap between the rocks at the mouth of the cave, he'd barricaded himself inside.

He was crawling around on all fours, she told us, sobbing, searching for cracks in the cave walls that might be permitting the wind. It was talking to him, and he didn't like it.

In terror, she watched him fit the last rock into place, his shadowy face slip-sliding from view.

The rescuers surmised that he'd exhausted himself carrying the fifty or so rocks that weighed twenty-five pounds each from the back of the cave to the front. I wonder if he changed his mind after sealing himself in like that. Maybe he tried to carry them back.

Then again, maybe not. Because when the crew blasted the entrance open, they discovered that he'd mixed his last drops of water with dirt to create mud seals between the rocks. Both his hands, now more like gnarled claws, were clasped over his ears. He went screaming, his mouth looking like a dog's bottom. The autopsy report said he died of dehydration.

But it was the wind, you see.

The traffic is heavy today. People continue fleeing the cities. Why do they head north? Don't they know they're driving straight into the jet stream?

I pump gas for the ones who are too afraid to get out and do it themselves. I make good money. I consider asking them for a ride, but I doubt it will be better anywhere else.

Mom and Dad refuse to leave. They grew up here. It took them thirty years to pay off their house. It's important to stick to your roots, they say. There's something beautiful about that, but I don't know what. I'm young, and I know there are things I don't know and can't touch. Maybe when I'm older. . . .

I finish filling up an SUV. Three small children sit in the back. They have big eyes. Someone's sealed the windows with duct-tape. It's futile, I want to tell them. But I don't.

I pump another tank, then another. The people need gas, and this is the only working station within fifty miles. The passengers stare at me like I'm a freak, a mutant, because I refuse to wear a mask. The drivers roll down their windows just enough to pay me. They never speak to me. I don't take it personally.

The air is calm today. That's rare.

Because for six months now, since the nukes destroyed most of the California coast, the wind has been our master, striking us like a whip, carrying invisible particles here, there, everywhere, all according to its whim. We are its slaves. Perhaps the gods are angry.

They say cancer is inevitable. It may take some time to form, but I'm definitely exposed. We all are, even the ones who run.

I won't run. And I won't wear the mask. I know they don't work.

Instead, I smile at the sun. I don't want to think about all that today.

I don't want to wonder about my father's cough. My

mother's sigh. How much time we have left.
  I save that for windy days.

Sheckley's Asylum

"ALRIGHT THEN, BRING IN THE WACKOS," SAID Sheckley.

Iris, the co-pilot, sighed. "Let's see who we got. Sector Seven's a strategic point, looks a little lax. We could add one more serial killer to the mix for every hundred thousand subjects. Should be enough to make the local news, maybe spike their adrenaline for a while."

Sheckley turned to the screen that was illuminated with flashing sector lights. Above the screen, through the cockpit window, revolved the blue planet. "One in a hundred thousand? Seems light. Not sure that's going to be enough. The parasites are getting stronger, and we have orders."

"Yeah, okay," she snapped.

"Add a mass murderer, too," Sheckley said. "Better

yet, two for the next three generations in Sector Seven. Start an urban legend, turn neighbors off from one another." He paused. "Let's make it one in fifty thousand. Something tells me we're going to need it."

"Couldn't hurt." Iris punched a few more buttons, set the coordinates for the DNA module, and continued scanning Sectors 1 through 797, looking for weak points where the parasites might get in.

Sheckley yawned and helped himself to another cup of coffee. These four o'clock slumps were always the hardest, even after thirteen years as a company man. He knew Iris felt them, too, after only five days on the job. He brought her her own cup without being asked, and set his creaking joints in the captain's chair.

"How'd that take?" he asked.

"Four generations in and looking strong. The parasites are staying far away from Sector 7."

"Good." He instinctively checked his watch again. "Thank God we're almost done. I'm getting hungry and—"

Beep. Beep.

Their eyes went to the white phone that was hanging up on the left side of the cockpit. And the little yellow button beneath it that blinked in time with the horrible noise. It could only mean one thing.

Iris groaned.

Sheckley shared the sentiment but said nothing. He thought of his wife, and how she was going to kill him if he was late again. He picked up the call and began speaking to their superior.

Iris watched blankly, expecting nothing good.

"I understand," Sheckley said. "Thank you." He hung up and faced Iris. "The parasites have found a way in."

"But that's impossible! I've searched every sector. All our analyses—"

"The poles, Iris."

"The what?" Her face dropped. "But they're guarded by miles of ice." She punched into Sector 49, the Antarctic region. "Oh."

Sheckley leaned in and pointed at the screen. "See? The humans heated things up too much, too fast. That's why we missed it."

"What do we do now?"

"Boss says for us to come in and debrief at the office. Another long night ahead of us. Damage control. Melissa's gonna be pissed." He popped a pain reliever.

Iris stewed. "Stupid humans."

"Crazy experiment, if you ask me. Gather every nut job in the galaxy and set them in Earth bodies; things are bound to get a little out of hand. Whoever thought using humans as intergalactic scarecrows was a good idea?"

Iris grinned. "I think you did."

"Hmm, that's right. Oh, well."

"Think we'll get fired for this?"

"Nah. It happens. Besides, it only took one work day to figure out humans don't ward off the parasites."

"Where do you think we'll go tomorrow?"

"Not sure." Sheckley buckled himself in, pulled the lever with his tentacle, and set their ship loose from Earth's moon. By the time he blinked his four eyes, the blue planet was a distant dot in their rearview mirror.

"Too bad when you think about it," he continued. "Man seemed perfect. They're easy to control, and implanting their DNA is simple stuff. Plus, they procreate quickly—7,500 generations in one work day."

Iris nodded and tried to relax, her fourteen barbed suckers stretching along the cockpit floor. "Yeah, what can you do, I guess."

"Let's stop in at Pluto. I got a hankering for an orc burger. My treat."

Iris brightened. Maybe this job had its perks after all.

Croakman

T HE PAST IS LIKE A FOSSIL THAT SHOULDN'T BE DUG up. Sometimes there are consequences. You really should let it be. Bones like to lie silently, you know?

Croakman? Why do you want to hear about him? Yeah, he lived up on Dinosaur Hill, in the one-story brick place with the oak tree and swing.

You'll have to speak up a little, I'm hard of hearing these days . . . Yes, you heard right. Many went crazy afterward. Most did.

What did they do wrong? Why did they go crazy?

No harm in telling you. I'm eighty-four now, and no one's gonna prosecute us. Hell, we're still considered heroes in most circles.

What are you so scared for? I'm just leaning in to

readjust myself. If you're gonna film this and we're gonna talk, I need to be comfortable. You don't trust me, you can take my bowie knife . . . There you go. Feels good in your hand, right?

Okay, then, "the practice." We heard about it from Solomon, a buddy of mine who grew up on Sycamore Valley Road, back when it was farmland. He'd heard about it from someone else, and I think it went all the way back to some foreign country long ago, who probably heard about it from someone else, and so on, and so on.

But we'll get to that. We'll get to the blood later.

Croakman, he lived up on the hill when the war broke out. He'd been one of the good ones, never going out of his way to hurt no one. He just minded his own business, wasn't involved in the revolution, or so we thought at the time.

Folks thought he was a little weird on account of his hunchback. You ever seen somebody with a *real* hunchback? I don't know if it's just a deformed spine that causes it, but it's like a camel's hump.

We'd gone up there that night to see about using his hill as a lookout point, set some folks up with binoculars who could see down into the valley. You got a 360-view of the town, and also of old Beckman Road, so it was easy to spy an ambush coming from the forest.

There were three of us that night: me, Joseph, and Red. We brought our guns, of course. You had to, back then.

The porch light came on. The door opened. There was Croakman.

His eyes, that was the other thing—those massive eyes that seemed to leap out at you from all directions. They *protruded* from his eye sockets. I could see the back halves of his eyeballs when he did that, and they were all yellow.

It was the damndest thing.

"Mr. Croakman," I said. "Us boys from the 43rd Regiment were wondering if you wouldn't mind us using your hilltop for a lookout, which would help us against the damn Martians."

His eyes bugged out again. Looked like he was thinking about something awful. Put the fear of God in me. But we had orders, and we needed that perch.

"I don't like to get involved, son." He had a heavy smoker's voice. Deep and scratchy and wheezy, but more exaggerated, like someone had run sandpaper down his throat.

Red stepped up behind me. He was the runt of us three, but only in height. "This is enemy-hiding territory, and the country sure as shit is taking sides. Choose wisely, old man." He spat on the porch. "Your country needs you."

Croakman stared at us. I could hear him wheezing.

I turned and looked over my shoulder. Joseph had stepped back; uneasy, I think. We all were, except for Red; he was a fighter. A bully. If he got scared of someone he would just get bigger and meaner. Soldiers—real ones—are like that.

"You with the Martians," Red asked, stepping up to Croakman, "or with us?" He peered into the house. He saw Croakman's daughter, Priscilla, back in the living room, and flicked his head at her. "What about you?"

Croakman stepped in front of him. "The Martians haven't hurt anyone."

"That a fact, old man? What about the young boys who got run over by them last month? Was in the news. In Arizona, yeah?"

"That's One-State propaganda, son."

Red turned to us, grinned. "He's with *them*. Selling out his own race." Then he whipped around and fake-lunged at Croakman. Trying to scare him. You know, kid stuff.

Croakman didn't move. Didn't even blink.

"How do we know you ain't hiding any of 'em in here now, huh?"

"I'm not."

Red held up the One-State declaration. "This says we're justified in entering the homes of any 'suspected sympathizers'."

"You can't come in."

"The government says I can, old man."

His daughter must have been getting nervous, because she backed up and bumped into the end table by the couch, the one that had the lamp on it. It fell on the floor. She yelped in surprise.

Red's hand instinctively pulled out the gun in his waistband. "Don't move, Priscilla."

Everything happened slowly—

Priscilla edging backwards.

Red hollering at her.

Another step back.

Croakman's eyes getting bigger.

One last warning from Red.

—and then all at once.

Croakman tried to slam the door, but Red barreled in anyway and knocked him down. The back of Croakman's head slammed on the hardwood with a heavy thud.

The girl froze. She wanted to run but didn't want to leave her father. Red made her decision easier. He caught her around the waist and tackled her to the floor.

I was the last one inside. Joseph had rushed to the old man and was kicking him in the gut with his steel-toed boots. Croakman's eyes bugged in and out of his sockets. Each kick seemed to push them out farther. Looked like he was in a kids' cartoon.

"Check the house!" Red yelled at me. He was busy tying up the girl.

I ran down the hall. It was lined with pictures of Croakman and his wife and daughter. Looked in the bedrooms, behind the beds, the closets. No Martians hiding there.

Then, on the bookshelf, something caught my eye. The collected writings of Orenshenko, one of the unofficial leaders of the Martian resistance.

Now, it wasn't illegal, strictly speaking, to have that particular book, but it was commonly known that reading their literature could turn normal-thinking Americans into Martian sympathizers. It'd been documented many times. It was one of the ways our soldiers would go turncoat on us.

I paused. I had to decide whether I would show the others. If I did, it would for sure mean death for Croakman and the girl. But if I didn't, I'd be, how you say, endorsing their behavior. That book might help someone sow discord in the future.

In the end, it didn't matter. Red and Joseph had already finished tying them up and were making the final preparations. When I showed them the book, their suspicions were confirmed.

I gathered the pictures on the walls and threw them in the hall closet. They shouldn't have to see the things we do.

I won't describe what Red did to the girl. Men do things in war.

Don't look at me like that. You weren't around then. You don't know what it was like.

What did you say? Do I regret it?

I don't like the question. You gotta understand, this thing is like inputs and outputs. Nothing more. That's all that governs human behavior. You with your college degrees or whatever else you got that makes you think you know something about people—you don't know shit. It's all theory with you.

We think in boxes. Say you're a fisherman, and you get paid for all the fish you bring in. The fish aren't fish no more. You look at them like they're *money* because catching them means you can buy food and keep a home and send your kids to college to read all those funny books about "people." And if the ocean's runnin' out of fish, you don't really care because you need them to make money for your family. You'll fish 'em right out of existence.

Or, say that the North American government declares war on the Martians. Say that it's our duty to root them out, and whatever happens don't count as crimes. They're justified because it's war, and all's fair in it. When you see a Martian, you don't *see* a Martian. You see a parasite, something that's gonna leech off you and your family. And the power of the state is behind you, telling you what the Martians are, and the state takes all the responsibility. No, actually, it's on the Martians themselves, for *being* Martians in the first place.

Then, you do what you do.

At the time, we did what the inputs told us to do.

And we didn't do nothing wrong.

AFTER WE'D FINISHED WITH THE GIRL, RED TOOK HER outside and ended it. That's all I have to say on the subject.

Croakman sat on the floor, hands behind his back.

The others, they didn't believe in "the practice"—in the power of the blood. But I made sure to drink a little, straight from the hearts. The best way to do this is to open up the chest and lick it. If you do that, you won't go crazy. It's an old superstition, but I believed it. Still do. Red and Joseph didn't. They didn't lick the hearts.

Joseph shot himself five or six years later. We lost touch after the war ended, but I heard he was having a hard time adjusting. The country was celebrating the victory, but he was off drinking. Someone found him up there on Dinosaur Hill, under the oak tree, covered in leaves. It was autumn.

Red hung on a long time, 'til about ten years ago when the government spilled the beans with their announcement. I don't know if Red felt guilty, necessarily, when he heard, but it definitely don't help one's state of mind to discover they played a part in destroying the world. Then again, who could have guessed the Martians had come to help us escape from this rock before the solar flare comes two years from now.

Do I feel guilty? You keep asking me the same thing. Why? Is it gonna change anything? No. So stop asking.

I wasn't the only one who did the killing—there were millions of us. That's why there's never been any war tribunals. We're all in on it, you got that? What does it matter now that the planet's almost dead?

Huh? You'll have to speak up. . . .

What happened to Croakman's wife?

Hell, I don't know. She was away on a trip at the time. She prolly remarried someone else after she heard the news. *Did she have more kids?* Word was, they were expecting at the time.

As for how old her grandkids might be, I don't know

that either. Prolly about your age. How old are you? Thirty-three? Sounds about right.

It's funny, but . . .

You kind of look like him a bit. Croakman. It's in the face. The shape of it . . .

Hey, be careful with that knife . . . It ain't something to play with . . .

Wait, what did you say your last name was?

And what's that you're doing with your eyes?

Still You Hear the Soldier Scream

I T'S THE FORTY-SEVENTH ANNIVERSARY OF THE START
of the ongoing Terran War, and this is one of those
events you'll tell your friends about for years. You're
annoyed, because this man is going to make you late for
work—he's standing in your way, after all, and your
office is *up there*, and why is he standing there screaming
like this?

You glance at the other people who have stopped to
watch. They wear dark slacks, nice shoes, like you. Hair
coiffed, like yours. None of you have ever seen a
screaming man like this. You sense a vague obligation to
help him—but for some reason, you don't.

You push to the front of the line for a better look.

The screaming man is wearing camo fatigues. He grips a briefcase. You see white in his knuckles.

And his face. Contorted. Veins and tendons strained through his pale-white skin. When he turns profile, you see his Adam's apple swelling like an oversized bulge in a man's tightie whities.

The One-State Army Bureau in downtown San Francisco is no building to scream at. You all know this. No one has to say it.

"He's been here an hour already," a gray-suited bureaucrat tells you as he munches a doughnut. A few of the onlookers make conversation. A strange bonding experience. Somehow you feel like old friends now. "Hasn't stopped once. Don't know how his voice can hold up that long."

Someone scans the screaming man's face and runs it through the Forum. Details emerge. His name: Joe Armstrong. A military man. A sergeant, a sixteen-year veteran. Three tours in the Great War. You whistle, amazed. It's a miracle he's survived this long. You only did one tour, which was compulsory then, and got out after two years.

Police lights. Sirens.

"Sir, I need to ask you to quiet down." The first officer, forty pounds of gear strapped around his waist, steps up to Sergeant Joe Armstrong, places one hand in front of his face. But Joe doesn't stop. Doesn't even notice him.

The officer tries again. "I'm going to give you a ticket for disturbing the peace!" No response. He steps away to confer with his partner and discuss their options. You doubt they've been trained for this.

The partner, a short, pudgy, bald guy who looks conspicuously out of place, tries his luck. They've got to

be civil here. Delicate, even. Too many people watching.
"Sir, I'm going to place you under arrest unless you stop
screaming. Do you understand?"

You glance up the side of the building. Coworkers
squash their faces against the glass as they peer down.

The soldier keeps screaming.

The officer removes the handcuffs from his belt. He
yanks on Armstrong's forearm, but it doesn't budge.
Instead, the soldier wobbles, stiff as dead wood, a
mannequin cast in stone. The officer yells at him to stop
resisting. When he doesn't, he is tackled to the ground.
You wince at the crack of his head.

Still, the soldier screams.

You turn. The crowd has grown. It's starting to spill
into the street, blocking traffic. The automatic cars have
stopped, too. It seems eerily quiet.

The second officer rushes to help the first. They flip
Joe onto his stomach and wrest his arms behind his back
without his permission. You hear a bone snap.

Unable to unwind his fingers from around the
briefcase handle, the officers bash them with their
batons. *Whap, whap, whap!* The fingers refuse to loosen.

The two cops back away, breathing heavily. A federal
security guard jogs up, hands them each industrial-grade
earplugs. They stick them in and decide what to do next.

Your stomach tightens, you're going to vomit. You
just know it. You whip around, kneel on the pavement,
and the sensation passes.

When you stand, a second security guard emerges
from the building holding a rag and a roll of duct tape.
The officers shove the rag into the screaming man's
mouth. When it's good and tight in there, they wrap the
tape twice around his head. The scream is stifled now,
but more guttural. Animalistic even.

Now, the briefcase. Your stomach lurches as the police resume whacking the screaming man's fingers. After three whacks, the fingers turn purple. They looked like abused sausages. After ten whacks, the knuckles shatter like walnut shells.

Still the man screams. Still he grips his briefcase.

More police, more sirens. Eight or nine officers now. They each take turns smashing Sergeant Armstrong's fingers. You overhear a female officer who hangs back—crowd control, you know—say the suitcase must be removed before they arrest him. There could be a bomb inside.

Woop, woop!

The bomb squad pulls up. In tow are more police, an ambulance, a fire truck. It's very crowded now. You shove people away. Don't want to lose your spot. A front-row view of this event is mandatory.

The robot steps out of the back of the police van. It's seven feet tall and walks on two legs. A technician controls it remotely. Its fingers are made of metal pincers. Its jet-black eyes conceal a dozen tiny cameras.

When it reaches the screaming man, it pauses. Cocks its head to the side, sizing him up. The screaming man pays it no attention.

The robot's metal pincers reach down and grip the man's index finger at the knuckle.

And they pull.

The finger is ripped backward from the hand, connected now by only a thin strip of flesh. Someone vomits as a fingernail skitters across the pavement.

The robot moves on to the other three fingers and the thumb, breaks them all. Then it drags the briefcase a safe distance away. The fingers look like scrabbling crab legs.

Police demand that you back up. You run to building-right and leap up onto the statue near the water fountain. This is your perch now.

A little door opens in the robot's abdomen, from which extends a whirring saw that severs the lock on the briefcase. The robot backs away. A technician appears wearing a puffy, protective suit. Kneeling by the case, he places his hands on the latches.

Pop! The briefcase springs open.

Silence.

The technician stares inside.

And withdraws a single piece of paper.

You crane your neck to see.

The words printed on it are big and black:

"LISTEN TO ME."

The screaming soldier has burst the capillaries in his face. His nose has been shattered. Looks like smashed bread. At his feet lie his crumbled teeth.

Still, he screams.

Someone starts the chant and slowly everyone picks it up, and suddenly you're chanting for the man, and it's growing louder and more intense, and it's not a chant anymore—it's a scream. You all scream for the screaming man.

"LISTEN TO HIM! LISTEN TO HIM! LISTEN TO HIM!"

You realize now the message of the screaming man. You all do. It's so obvious.

There is no message.

The scream is the message.

The police turn on the crowd. They yell into walkie talkies. They fan out, then encircle you all. *Time to go home. Show's over.*

Someone strikes an officer in the head with a rock.

He staggers, falls, and the others respond immediately with tear gas and rubber bullets. You feel a tug on your arm. You look down. You've been hit. You cover the back of your head and flee down the road through the smoke that's sprung up like a magician's trick. Eyes burning, throat aflame, you retreat to an alley, hustle through to the next street, and sprint to the police station.

There you wait for the screaming man to be delivered. You can hear him even before he's led out of the police car, a sort of low-pitched growl-yell behind the rag.

The officers drag the screaming Joe Armstrong through the front door. Walking on his own is impossible. He screams while they book him. He screams when they strip-search him. He screams as they lug him down the hall past the other inmates.

Later, inmates and officers who were willing to talk tell you what happened. Joe Armstrong was retching, gagging on the wet, grimy cloth that had been shoved into his throat. In their cells, the other inmates smashed pillows over their ears, flushed their toilets repeatedly. Nothing could stifle the sounds.

The guards soon grew weary. After three hours, the screaming produced such an acute anxiety in them that they were unable to hold down solid food. They had no choice but to do what they did. The posse of twelve cops marched to the man's cell. They tried once more to speak some sense into him. When that didn't work, they tried fists. When that didn't work, they tried clubs.

Finally, a shot rang out. Then another. The man who screamed screamed no more. The body mysteriously disappeared some time later. There is no record of an autopsy. You've checked.

The death is pronounced a "suicide by cop." The

Army sends the screaming veteran's family a folded flag.

Two decades pass. The country has been at war with Terra for sixty-seven years. No protests to bring the troops home have worked. Nor has pleading with Congress, or letters to the president. And every year, more and more soldiers march up to the One-State Army Bureau to scream. This year, thousands will come. They will stand outside the building and wail. They will carry briefcases with one-sentence messages scrawled on slips of paper. They will be beaten and put to death.

It's easy to see what they want.

But their message is never heard.

Wreckoning

SIGHT

ON HIS TWELFTH BIRTHDAY, CHARLIE WEBB'S parents decided it was time for him to see what it meant to be an adult, so they made the appointment to give him his eyes.

Born with congenital cataracts, Charlie had never seen his parents, their home, or the sun that had become increasingly reddened by the synthetic Martian atmosphere. His parents, who had great health benefits, were able to get him the procedure at a lower price than most.

At home, they unwrapped the bandages from around his head. Charlie squinted, getting used to the light. In his blindness, he hadn't seen *nothing*. He had seen colors and streaks, here and there. His parents always told him that was normal for the blind. Something about synapses and protein strands.

"Is that the bookshelf?" he asked after the unwrapping, putting visuals to the items he'd groped at in the dark for his entire life. He spent three days gazing at everything, especially the hover cars that zoomed outside their windows.

And all was fine and good, and their family was as fine and good as could be.

GREMLINS

TWO WEEKS LATER, CHARLIE AND HIS MOM WERE TAKING a stroll around their neighborhood. Each large home had a lawn manicured by tiny robotic insects. As they returned, Charlie pointed to something at the base of their house. "What's that?"

"What? I don't see anything," said Mrs. Webb.

"Right there! It's an animal or something."

"Oh, that. That's nothing." She waved her hand and kept walking.

"But it's chewing up the bottom of the house."

Mrs. Webb took his hand and told him not to worry so much, that it wasn't good for his health. She unlocked the door with the retina scanner, and they went inside. Soon, Charlie forgot all about the small creature.

That night, as he was trying to sleep, he heard

something *scratch-scratch-scratching* on the side of the house. Peeking out his second-story window, the wind flash-chilling his skin beneath his pajamas, he spied the same red creature he had seen earlier, low to the ground, scurrying along the base of the house on all fours.

Charlie craned his neck for a better look. Everywhere the creature went its jaw clanked up and down, up and down, splintering the wood panels. Then it set its mouth sideways, walking along, nibbling away.

Charlie shut the window and tried to sleep. Mom had said not to worry. But how long would they eat the house for?

MRS. WEBB POURED HER SON A GLASS OF ORANGE JUICE and set it alongside his eggs and toast. She took her own plates to the sink and washed them. "There's your father again," she said, shaking her head, peering out the kitchen window into the backyard.

Yep, there was Charlie's papa alright. Already in his rocking chair, looking out over the golf course they lived on—the ninth-hole green.

"What's he holding?" asked Charlie.

"His shotgun, silly."

Charlie's eyes gleamed. He'd heard many stories about the gun—heard it go off many times, but—

"Can I play with it?" he asked.

His mom sighed. "I suppose. Go ask your father."

Moments later, Charlie was standing next to his dad. Mr. Webb didn't look at him. He just rocked in his chair, back and forth, watching the golf course. He rocked for quite a long time.

His father rarely spoke to him. But Charlie often spoke to his dad; he knew his dad liked it. He'd told him so, once. So Charlie sat and asked questions, and Mr.

Webb didn't respond but that was okay.

Every so often, Mr. Webb would yell into the air and fire his shotgun. The noise was loud, but at least now Charlie would know it was coming. Unlike before, when he had only the short warning of the pump. The very mention of the gun was enough to tighten his neck and shoulders and invoke intense bodily shaking.

The doctors sometimes called that stress.

Mr. Webb racked the gun. An empty shell landed behind him on the small pile of shells that had accumulated there. Beads of sweat lined his forehead. He looked pained.

"I got the cancer," he said. "I got it bad."

"No, you don't, Dad. You've been saying that since I was a baby."

Mr. Webb ignored him. "It's in my stomach. It's working its way into my liver and kidneys. I can feel it growing. You'd think in the year 2158 we'd have a cure, but I guess not." He stared off for a long while. Somewhere a golf club struck a ball.

Suddenly, he shrieked like an animal in agonizing pain. Again he fired the shotgun into the air.

Charlie watched the discharged shell fall onto the growing pile. His vision drifted past the pile, to one of the creatures gnawing at the base of the house. He could see it had already eaten a six-inch hole into the wood; soon it would be able to crawl under their home.

Charlie asked his father about them.

"Huh? Those are nothing. Don't worry about them. They're just doing their job."

"What job?"

But Mr. Webb shrieked again and shot his gun into the air three times. "I got the cancer," he said.

Charlie sighed, and returned to the house.

MISGIVINGS

CHARLIE COULDN'T HAVE GUESSED MATILDA WAS SO pretty. By society's arbitrary standards, she was not. She had a weak chin and a square head, and never grew out of either. She walked duck-footed. But when Charlie saw her his first day back at school, he grew shy and found it hard to speak.

"Do you see colors now, too?" she asked.

"Yes, I think so."

She held up a forest green marker. "What color is this?"

"Blue."

"That's right!"

Then it was time for the children to line up at their desks, where they stood for thirty minutes each day while the teacher got herself sorted out.

Charlie had always heard the sounds of Ms. Temple's self-flagellation, and was curious about what exactly happened during those periods of intense whacking and crying.

Now he got to see. Ms. Temple was slamming the end of a long ruler against her forehead, over and over. The whap left red streaks. This went on for fifteen minutes until the timer went off.

She took a deep breath before whipping out a small mirror and redoing her makeup.

Sammy Finkelstein, a short boy with glasses and brown curls, yawned. It made Charlie yawn. All the children yawned.

At that moment, Matilda's hand grazed Charlie's. He looked at her. She half-smiled but didn't look back.

"All eyes on me!" yelled Ms. Temple. "It's time for our weekly Misgivings." Some groans went up. "Anthony Vasquez!"

The boy named Anthony sighed, stared at his shoes.

"You're still playing baseball, yes?"

Anthony nodded.

"Right or left-handed?"

"Right, Ms. Temple."

"Okay, then."

Anthony stepped up to Ms. Temple and turned profile to her. She punched him on the right arm three times.

"But I have to pitch today," he protested, massaging his bicep.

"That's the whole point!" Ms. Temple flung him around and sent him back into line. Her face crinkled. She seemed to be in discomfort. She dug through her purse and quickly swallowed three extra-strength pain relievers. "I'm going to get diabetes, I just know it," she said to no one in particular and took a big bite from a piece of cake on her desk.

Charlie stared at the cake. It was decadent and triple-layered and had icing with pearls on top. He watched Ms. Temple finish her bite, shake her head at herself in disgust, then dig in for another. When she was done, her face sagging with anguish and heavy cream, she grabbed her stomach and lifted herself out of her seat to continue the Misgivings.

She called little Alicia Evans to the front. Alicia was smart, maybe the smartest in the whole class. Ms. Temple made her stand on her head for fifteen minutes until she nearly passed out.

Then it was Matilda's turn. Ms. Temple looked her up and down and decided, like every week, that Matilda had enough wrong with her, that there was no reason to impair her further, and sent her back to the line—but not before berating her for all the things wrong with her, and warning that if she was ever going to be someone she'd better learn to fix them.

Beaming, Matilda returned to the line. She is so beautiful, Charlie thought.

"Charlie!" yelled Ms. Temple. "You can see now, correct?"

"Yes, Ms. Temple. But no better than anyone else. In fact, the doctor said I see a little less good than most people."

"Hmm." She leaned back, tried to find something, but seeing as how she couldn't find anything wrong that set him apart physically from the rest of the class, she decided not to punish him that way today.

She did, however, yell at him about the color of his eyes.

As Charlie walked back into line, he and Matilda shared a snicker. She touched his hand.

Upon seeing them touch, Ms. Temple flew into such a rage that she sprinted to the school kitchen for another massive piece of cake. When she returned, she shoved half of it down her throat. She gasped for air, wheezing and gurgling. Her red, bleary eyes bulged in menacing alarm. Snot flew from her nose.

When she was finished, she screamed into the little intercom on her watch, made the necessary arrangements, and soon two agents whisked Charlie out of the classroom.

He was transferred to another school a few blocks away, where the authorities were sure he and Matilda wouldn't speak. Their child-love had set them apart from their classmates—had elevated them too much. If only they'd kept it secret.

His parents weren't angry, of course. These things happened. His own mother, that day in fact, had been demoted from her position as project manager at the nuclear plant for no reason except that it was her turn. Her pay decreased by fifteen percent.

WRECKONING

THAT WEEKEND, WHILE CHARLIE WAS SITTING IN THE backyard, about twenty yards from the house, he heard the wood creaking. He'd been watching the gremlins with the steel teeth chomp at the baseboards of his home. There were more today, maybe two dozen of them.

Every now and then a golf ball would whiz by on the course. If it was a bad shot, the golfer would sigh with relief. If it was good, well, the curses Charlie heard were not meant for such young ears.

When the gremlins finished eating the foundation of the house, it leaned to one side and fell, shattering the neighbor's fence. (A lawsuit, no doubt about that.) Charlie dove behind the old oak tree to avoid the shrapnel.

When it looked like the dust was settled, and all of the family's belongings were busted, flattened, or covered in dust and asbestos, Charlie walked up to one of the gremlins that was pedaling its feet sideways on the ground. Its back legs had been partially crushed by the falling home. Charlie absentmindedly kicked the little beast. The loose metal springs in its synthetic belly sprang sideways and onto the grass. Its jaw opened and shut with a snap—then its gears slowly ground down and all was quiet.

Charlie's parents arrived a few minutes later. Mr. Webb stood with his hands on his hips and said, "Alright, who's hungry?"

They went out for pizza. They laughed and joked. It was the happiest night of their lives.

For the next six months, they lived out of a hotel while their home was rebuilt. Mr. Webb oversaw the reconstruction effort, each day whistling as he drove to the site, cleaned up the rubble, and directed the architects and the contractors and carpenters. He'd never been so full of joy. He felt like a new man.

And when it was done, he stood with his family in the shade of a peach tree he'd planted in the front yard. They marveled at their new home, filled with pride and a sense of achievement.

The gleam in his eye lasted only a moment. Charlie watched as his face dropped. The life seemed to fade from him.

Mr. Webb shook his head. "I've got lung cancer. It's the dust from the house. I can feel it in my body." He sighed. "It's too late for me. I just know it."

A breeze from the synthetic atmosphere blew through Charlie's hair. His father looked at him, a tear running down his face. He collapsed on the ground in racking sobs.

And that was how Charlie learned to be an adult in this world. Now he could really see.

The Cosmos of Meaning

ELLIOT HAD BEEN SEEING DOUBLE ON AND OFF FOR A week, feeling woozy and disconnected from his surroundings. The Terran doctor looked him up and down, kneaded his tummy while peering through shining instruments, then sent him upstairs to the neurologist, who also found nothing wrong. Elliot was sent home with some benzodiazepine in case what was diagnosed as severe anxiety was to return.

He awoke the next day nervous as ever. Amid swirling thoughts, he rushed into the forest near his home and tramped right off the path so he could find some peace and quiet. He could no longer hear anything except what was inside his head. At some point, he fell to his knees and began weeping.

When he was finished, he looked up and blushed. An older gentleman was resting not ten feet from him, legs up, lying back on a naturally inclining tree stump that had been split down the middle. The man looked quite comfortable.

Elliot rose, wiped his nose, and shoved his hands in his pockets. He stood there awkwardly. He wore blue jeans, now covered in mud, and shoes resembling those worn by teenagers on Terra. He silently chastised himself and resolved to throw them in the trash and buy another pair. Something more adult, yes.

"Ssh," the man said, grinning, one hand signaling Elliot to remain silent, head cocked, listening to the sounds of the—

"Albino parakeet," the man said. "Rare these days." He smiled and jotted something in his notebook. "You almost drove it away. It's the last species of bird I had to document in these woods. So glad I finally finished."

And as sometimes happens between two strangers who stumble across each other in the middle of the woods, they talked for some time until the subject of Life emerged, and Elliot, feeling comfortable with this strange man who wore a scarf and smoked a pipe, let the innards of his mind spill onto the forest floor.

"I don't know what's happening to me," he said. "I have a wonderful job as a writer. I live in my favorite city. I have plenty of money. I'm freer than I've ever been in my whole life, but I'm anxious all the time. I feel like I'm not living at all. I can't sleep, my head spins a million miles a minute. Everything is wonderful on the outside, but on the inside I'm a complete mess. I'm so indecisive, even trying to figure out what to make for dinner is like negotiating peace talks with Martian rebels. I just keep asking myself what's wrong, and I have no good answer. Does that make sense?"

"Perfect sense."

"I can't even have a normal conversation with friends. The second I step out into the street, I start hyperventilating. I'm having an existential crisis, that's it. Or I'm going crazy. I can't tell which."

The old man nodded, then lay back onto the log. "Tell me more."

"Living life feels like I'm just playing a role. Always pretending to be something. When I was young, I had to step up and be the hero and take care of everyone because my father was a drunk, and I've read that's what happens sometimes in families like mine. But I know that's not who I actually was deep down. It's just who I needed to be at the time.

"And then I went to school. But I was just playing another role based on who I thought I was supposed to be, or who I thought *others* thought I was supposed to be, to get along, to get good grades, make a living, whatever. I was a class clown for a while, tried to wear the right clothes, date the right person. And it didn't stop after school. The roles followed me into my job. I went to law school and got a degree, and I hate law!

"It's like we assign ourselves these roles because we need them in order to live in society and make money, or have friends, or be a part of a group. I even got married once because I *thought* I should. I met her at a job where I *pretended* to be outgoing and extroverted—and it was all fake. Look where that got me!"

Elliot took a deep breath. "So when I realized this, it made me think—'Who am I?' And I freaked out!"

"I'll bet!" said the old man.

"But now all I see are masks. Personas. What's real? What's real about *anything* we do? Am I crazy?"

"That depends on who you ask. What you're experiencing is a kind of break from society's rules. A schism. By refusing to play the game, you're leaving the collective delusion of society."

"Is that it?"

"Possibly. But let's back up. Your idea is an interesting one, so let's use an example we can both relate to: family. Why is it so draining to be around family for long periods of time? I believe it's because each family member has joined this group called 'family' and is now supposed to play a role in it, even if it's not who they truly are. Each family has its own story, and that abstract idea must be upheld or else the 'family' falls apart. This is different than the family's biology, mind you. This is about a story. It's not limited to families, either. It's true of any group, including our overall society.

"So, in one sense, you are experiencing a type of insanity. Society's rules are a way of keeping things organized, and you are consciously choosing to dis- organize them by refusing to wear a mask. And when people refuse to join the collective, they are placed in asylums or treatment centers, whereby after a time they may be allowed to rejoin society. Which is another way of saying they are being allowed to rejoin society's *delusions*, its constructs, its abstractions.

"But on the other hand, you are absolutely sane. The ego of our world *is* a mask, and societies wear them just as individuals do. The question is: what do you do about that?"

"Yes! What *do* I do?"

"Do you want the real answer?"

"Sure."

"You won't like it, but I'll tell you anyway. Are you ready?"

"Come out with it already, man."

"Okay, then," said the man named Sartre the 57th. "My answer is that I don't know what you should do. You are condemned to freedom."

"Huh? Condemned to freedom? What does that even mean?"

"It means you're responsible for what you do."

"That doesn't feel like freedom, much less freedom from any of society's delusions."

"You're right. It doesn't. Freedom requires responsibility. And responsibility doesn't feel free. It feels like responsibility. What you're describing—your anxious state—is your waking up to *freedom.* You have seen beyond the masks, and that's important. You are free from the delusions you previously *chose* to believe."

"But I didn't *choose* to believe in any of this," Elliot protested. "I was just a child when I learned society's delusions or whatever you call them."

"That's right. If you think about it, you really don't choose much in this life. Nobody chooses their parents, their generation, the society they're born into. Nobody chooses their DNA, their biological looks, their innate gifts, even.

"However, we do choose our own actions in any given situation—even if at the time we felt like we had no choice. Sure, we can tell ourselves we *had* to leave our spouse, or cheat on a test, or buy a home, but the truth is we always choose our actions."

"I call bullshit on that," Elliot said. "Are you saying that slaves made a choice to be slaves? That children, poisoned by chemicals, are *choosing* to be poisoned?"

"Absolutely not. I am only describing attitudes and actions. For example, let's say I'm accused of wizardry and am locked up. I'm unable to leave my cell, so I have only a few options. I can choose to do my time quietly or try to break out or go on a hunger strike. I didn't choose my getting locked up, but I do have a choice about what do now, yes?"

The old man stretched, yawned. "Now, your situation. You are free-floating. You have no real problems that I can see. On the outside, all seems well."

"Yes. But what's the point of it all? If all we do is try to get along with our masks, and assign fake roles to fake people so we can live comfortably—what *is* the point? What do I *do*?"

"I already told you. I don't know what you should do."

"That's not an answer."

"Of course it is. Choices are the chains of freedom. Understand? You have to make your own decisions. But I'll give you a hint, which is only a hint and not an answer.

"If you've stripped away the masks of society and have found the truth—which is that there is *NOTHING* beneath the masks—then it's your duty to go into the emptiness and find *meaning*.

"The point of life is not, as some people say, to be happy. Rather, it is to find meaning in the vast emptiness of life. It is paradoxical, maybe, but you must find *meaning in the meaninglessness*. You must. It's your responsibility now, as a free person."

"But I didn't ask for this responsibility. I don't want it."

"Who cares what you did or did not ask for? You

choose little in your life, as we've already established. But it is *your* life, and you must take responsibility for it—unless, of course, you choose not to do anything about it, which is perfectly all right if that's what you *choose* and are willing to bear the responsibility for your non-choice.

"Your journey into meaning—and meaninglessness—is a solo one. No one can, or should, make meaning for you. That's why I say I have no answers. Meaning is located somewhere in the void, so no two people find it in the same place. The search is lonely and chaotic and alienating, but that is life. It isn't good or bad, it's just the way life is."

Elliot sighed. "Okay, I have a problem though. When you talk about responsibility, it sounds an awful lot like you're talking about personal responsibility, like those assholes on the Forum who rail against poor people."

"I'm not commenting on anybody's personal situation. Life *situations* cannot be qualified in those ways, though commentators like to try. I'm only saying that everybody—regardless of their life situation, regardless of their position in this collective delusion we call society—has the power to choose their attitudes and actions and the meaning of their own lives. That's all."

"Fair enough. Now, about my—"

"Yes, about you. I've noticed you care an awful lot about yourself."

"Well, why shouldn't I? It's my life, isn't it?"

"Yes, it is. And it's important to care about oneself. You can't do much for others if your own house is burning down. However, given your present situation, I doubt you'll find much meaning—for your*self*—by paying so much attention to your*self*."

"That seems paradoxical. Isn't that where you'd find

meaning?"

"Perhaps. But many people who are focused on *self*-improvement—who take workshops and meditation retreats and food detoxes—to improve them*selves*—are some of the saddest people I know. Most of the time they end up using those activities to strengthen their masks rather than to transcend them, and therefore become more enslaved to them*selves* than ever before. They make 'self-improvement'—which is named that for a reason—an end in itself, and what meaning do you expect to find by constantly improving your mask? Those people are only creating barriers to their own emptiness, and what point is there in that?"

"So what I do is . . ."

"That is your freedom, and it's yours to figure out. I would never want to take that from you. But I'll tell you what I've observed about you from our conversation so far.

"You spend an awful lot of time thinking about yourself. You're looking at the ground when there is a whole world in front of you. And above you. Perhaps your answer is in the stars.

"If you want to find meaning—which is to say, *to see it*—you should try to create meaning for someone else. Then you will know it, for you will see the effects."

"And how do I do that?"

"First, remember that no two people find meaning in the same way. What you dismiss every day as meaningless may actually mean quite a lot to someone else who is navigating the emptiness. You never know where and when meaning will strike. Also, remember that most people don't know they're traveling through the emptiness. They have mistaken the collective delusion for something meaningful. So tread lightly.

Providing meaning is a gift; don't expect anything in return from anyone. Your reward is finding your own purpose. You don't need anything else.

"Start by being kind. Open doors. One smile can change someone's entire day. Or it may not. Doesn't matter. And remember, it's none of your business what other people think of you.

"You've been given this gift of seeing the reality of our emptiness. So use your knowledge wisely. You might decide to shatter people's illusions, and that would be quite painful for them. Alternatively, you could choose to let them live as they have been. And that's okay, too.

"Because here is my point, and the *only one you should pay attention to*: nobody can make your choices for you, and they shouldn't, because creating your own path and meaning in the meaninglessness of life is the only freedom you or anyone else has. *We are condemned to freedom.*"

Sartre the 57th patted Elliot on the shoulder. They sat there for some time. When Elliot looked up, night had fallen. Stars dotted the skyscape. There was nothing between the stars, he noticed, nothing at all.

The realization came on slowly and then all at once. And suddenly he saw his own meaning of Meaning, which was to be like a star in the vast emptiness of space. From his light, and the lights of others like him, people might draw their own maps and locate themselves in time and space. There was no single Meaning, no one way; there were only constellations. There was no way to know what others would see. The most he could do was shine and hope for the best.

When he felt it was time to go, he looked up to thank Sartre the 57th. But he found himself alone, and that was okay, because that's the way these things are supposed to be.

Head Shows

T HE CRAWLERS, WITH TIRES THE HEIGHT OF BOOTED
men, were ripping apart the earth. Alicia watched
them from the thirty-third story of the high-rise
in South San Francisco.

Work was slow today. Idly, she picked at a hangnail as
she copied and pasted text from one computer
application to another. Three weeks were left on her
contract; pretty soon her position would be automated,
and she'd be back in the pool of candidates in the ever-
dwindling job pile that still existed in and around Silicon
Valley.

She hid behind her cubicle wall and checked her
account on the Forum. So-and-so was getting married,

her childhood friend was raising money for medical bills, and her cousin had posted another meme about how stupid the president had been about that thing that happened a few days ago.

Outside, the machines continued to plunder.

When six o'clock came, Alicia left work and rode the train home. She stuck in her earbuds and listened to Arthur DeSantos rail against conservatives, unionization, and anti-abortionists. She agreed with him on all fronts and wondered who among the hundred people around her was as knowledgeable as she.

When she finished DeSantos's talk, she rated it ten out of ten on the Forum, posted it so everyone could see she was doing her part to spread his message, then stepped off the train and walked home.

She entered her apartment, keeping her head down as she passed Lucas's room—which consisted of makeshift walls of sheets in the living room—walked down the hallway past Micah and Mikaela's shared room, and Rashida and Violet's shared room, and into her own at the end of the hall where she plopped onto her bed.

Outside, the machines raged on. She felt a slight rumble as one tore down a building half a block away. She heard glass and concrete falling like heavy blankets on the streets and sidewalks. A haze of dust would consume everything in a two-block radius. The machines never stopped.

At 7 p.m., her tablet beeped. Time for their house meeting. Alicia had been dreading this all week. Not only had Rashida not done her dishes again, but they'd had an argument on the Forum for all to see about a meme Rashida had posted that ridiculed Angela Hart, the newscaster at the One-State News Network. Alicia had fired back that ONN's journalists were defenders of One-

State surveillance, and how dare they embolden the unionized separatists. The whole thing had turned nasty; they hadn't spoken since, not even when they'd bumped into each other in the hallway the night before.

So the residents of the 900-square-foot Unit 42A at the One-State Housing Building #279Q gathered for their meeting. It was Micah's turn to lead. "Lucas, the pathway to the kitchen has been cleared for the past month. Thank you for that. Namaste."

Everyone put their hands together and placed them over their heart. "Namaste."

"Now, the bad news. They're raising the rent again. This time by twelve percent."

"But that's the third time this year," Mikaela said. "They can't do that."

Rashida shook her head. "I already pay 75% of my income in rent. How can they expect *more*?"

"We don't have any rights," Alicia said. "They can do whatever they want."

"Well, we need to organize, tell them no. Someone has to tell them no. They're probably doing this to everyone on the block."

Boom. Outside, the thirty-foot crawlers leveled another building, the collapsing debris triggering a car alarm.

"Look," Micah said. "Either we pay them, or the Development Team is gonna bulldoze the building, just like every other place. They have no reason to keep it up. The Company will always want to pay them to tear it down. They can get more money that way."

"Let's throw ourselves in front of the tractors," Rashida declared, standing. The place erupted in argument.

Alicia stayed silent. She'd lost all respect for Rashida.

How could she protest next to *her*, with all her horrible opinions? Rashida rode a hydrogen scooter, for God's sake.

Alicia glanced from one face to the next. She had a set of principles to live by, and how could she possibly trust Lucas when he still listened to conservative radio shows on the Forum?

Then there was Violet, who was so far to the left as to be impractical. Micah had no larger goals except to have children, which made Alicia gag. Mikaela, well—just, no.

The meeting adjourned on Rashida's advice to reconvene the next day and figure out a plan to convince the electronic landlords of One-State to change their minds.

ALICIA'S FAVORITE HEAD SHOW WAS CALLED "IMAGINE the Space." It aired once a week on the Forum. She liked to listen in complete silence. When something disturbed her listening, she became highly agitated, so she often booked a meeting room at work where she could be alone. If that wasn't available, she would rush home and savor it on her bed.

The morning after the house meeting, she resumed her normal routine: wake up, turn on the Forum on her earbuds to hear what she'd missed while sleeping, and get ready for work. It was especially helpful then, because it blocked out Lucas's snoring and Mikaela's occasional singing in the shower.

From there, Alicia would walk to the train station while browsing head shows chosen by the Forum specifically for her and programmed for times of day most appropriate for her mood. Like most people, Alicia had synchronized her head shows with her mood tracker, which also integrated data like blood pressure and heart rate and could even predict serotonin levels.

She left the apartment this morning, sidestepping the unfortunate people who slept on the sidewalk. A homeless man held out his hand, which she successfully ignored by putting her sunglasses on at just the right moment and turning up the volume on her show.

"The One-State Council is recommending all unionization efforts be squashed immediately, and I couldn't agree more," said the host. "These workers are sick. Their leader just called Congresswoman Williams a sellout and refused to back her plan on trade. Let the unions fall, why should we help them anyway . . ."

Alicia felt a new, steely attitude spring up inside her. Yes, this was a new line in the sand. She made a mental note. The workers' bad attitude was a good argument against unionization. She must not forget it.

What does Neal think about that? she wondered. She'd have to remember to ask him later during their lunch date at work. She hoped he was on the right side of the issue. She liked him; they seemed to vibe on other topics.

Dating had been tough for her since she'd moved from Illinois to San Francisco. She couldn't seem to find anyone who shared her values. Every time she'd removed her earbuds for a couple hours to meet up with some new man for tacos or a movie, she'd been disappointed.

The first order of business in dating, she'd soon decided, was always to establish the zone of politics. In fact, it was the main way the Forum's Dating Algorithm matched people up. It had successfully led to the marriages of over half a million people.

Alicia stepped through the turnstile at the train

station, the credits subtracting and syncing from her implant to the station's computers. She boarded her train and stomached the cramped conditions.

Outside her destination, a fifty-foot crawler was busily ripping apart windows and brick and plaster, snarling like a mechanical beast, digging its way inside the building where it could pinch and grab and rip at its guts. To raze what was standing was its only aim. Once the crawlers were given a duty, they carried it out. It was all in the programming.

The sensor beeped and the door to the office opened. Alicia sat at her station, suddenly feeling very old and small, as if all the energy had been sucked out of her on the way in. (In fact, it had. The city was designed to sap the population's vitality.)

Alicia copied and pasted until noon, watching the crawlers as they chomped and cleared the structures. Past them, she could see other buildings being rebuilt. After demolition, new construction always went up. In this way, the economy of creation and destruction was extended indefinitely.

SITTING AT THE TABLE ALONE, ALICIA NERVOUSLY checked her watch. She was supposed to meet Neal for sushi during her lunch break. It wasn't like him to be late, and now they only had forty-seven minutes to spend together. Every minute she was late for work she would be docked pay, and with the imminent rent increase she needed all the income she could get.

Neal arrived with thirty-three minutes to spare. He apologized and wiped the sweat off his face with a handkerchief he kept in the breast pocket of his blazer. Alicia was hungry, and she ordered, tight-lipped. Neal apologized again, to no response.

The mechanical arm reached out of the floor and dropped a plate onto their table. Alicia stifled her sobs. They'd received nigiri, not sashimi. The credits had already been deducted from her account, so she had to open a Help Desk message with the restaurant's Forum page, but with no one to speak to she had to wait online for fifteen minutes, only to discover that they had no sashimi today and she'd have to eat the nigiri—though they did give her half off her next purchase. She gave the credits to Neal and watched him eat. With only a few minutes to spare, she abruptly asked him what he thought about the unionization issue.

He swallowed his fish and told her.

A few minutes later, she returned to work alone.

THE COMPANY-WIDE MEETING WAS AT I P.M. ALICIA arrived at the office at 12:58 p.m., which gave her just enough time to use the bathroom. They'd know if she was late to the meeting, too, because her implant with the small GPS inside would tell them.

The CEO's face appeared big and bloated on the screen that acted as a head for the robotic body underneath. The CEO was in Florida. He controlled the humanoid body from there.

Behind him, outside, a crawler tore down another building.

"Lastly," the CEO said, "I want to bring our attention to an important issue that affects us all. As you all know, the debates over miner unionization have reached a fever pitch. We've decided to join our sister company, Geneva Corp, who is standing with their efforts. We're going to be donating two hundred thousand credits. I hope you're proud to be working at a company that . . ."

When he was finished, the place erupted in cheers.

Alicia quit that afternoon.

SHE RETURNED HOME TO FIND HER FIVE ROOMMATES suiting up for battle. They had covered themselves in black garb from head to toe. Rashida said nothing to Alicia as she zipped up her hoodie and threw her backpack on.

Outside, the crawler tore into another building.

"You coming?" Lucas asked. "The Forum's Help Desk says there's nothing we can do. None of us can afford the rent increase. We think they're gonna tear this place down in the next few weeks. We're going out to protest. You in?"

Alicia looked at her roommates with contempt. These were not her people. She'd find others.

She shook her head no and went to her room. She listened to head shows, ate dinner, and went to bed, baffled and saddened after seeing her father's post on the Forum about his support of the unionization effort. When he called her that night, she declined to answer and went to sleep.

MICAH AND MIKAELA WERE THE FIRST TO MOVE OUT. At first they tried to find replacement tenants, but no applicants had income sufficient for the Forum's rent algorithm.

Violet moved back to New Seattle, and a few days later Lucas decided to return home to his folks. So it was just Alicia and Rashida.

Alicia spent her time trying to find another job. She was able to patch together some income as a part-time elder care specialist, a job that automation had not yet touched. Joining that line of work was easier than it had been in the past—many elders had dementia and Alzheimer's, and with so many patients, the qualifications for caretakers were a mere formality. They consisted of a simple test of being able to lift forty-five pounds over one's head, as well as a written exam and sworn testimony that you wouldn't steal from the patients. All medications were doled out into cups by machines. Shifts were only three hours long, and workers could come and go as they pleased.

The job paid almost enough to cover her groceries.

She had no luck finding another apartment in the city. And she wasn't the only one. Reports on the housing crisis flooded the Forum. Experts deduced that the algorithm had determined it was more profitable to tear down most of the apartments in the city and build new housing facilities that could each sleep hundreds of people. Other buildings would be used for storing military weapons. The western seaboard had become increasingly important to the defense industry since One-State had declared war on Two-State.

Alicia peeked through the living room curtains and saw the crawler walking toward her like an alien in a horror film. She'd received a warning from the Forum alarm system that her building would be demolished today.

She pressed her head against the window and peered down the street. A crowd had gathered nearby; some people waved signs, and others wielded long ropes they tried to wrap around the crawlers' legs to trip them up and bring them down. They were Leftists. Alicia could see that from the signs they carried.

She saw Rashida down there too, and felt something like pity and sorrow, not for them but for herself.

The crawler reached her building. Its claw broke

through her window, clamped down, and pulled away most of the living room floor. Alicia sat and waited for the crawler to take her with the rest of her home.

For what was the point of living if not to be right?

See You in Theaters

CHAPTER 1

WE'D BEEN IN THE HOUSE SIX MONTHS OR SO WHEN I discovered the two-foot-high door hidden behind the dresser in my bedroom. It's naturally very dark in there—there's only one small window—so you'd never see it unless you got lucky like I did banging into it on accident. It's one of those false doors with no handle and only opens when you push in the right place.

I stuck my head in and shined my flashlight around.

It was hot and dark inside. Ahead of me stretched a tunnel a few feet long, and then it dropped off toward the earth. The sides of the tunnel were made of metal, maybe aluminum. I started crawling.

I live in a neighborhood called Los Feliz, in Los Angeles. It's nice here. We're on the east side, which means that I'm not near the ocean, but the traffic isn't so bad, and there are concerts and films and all kinds of fun things to do. I'm only seventeen, but I can sneak some drinks from the bars, depending on the night.

My father works at a large corporation. I won't say which one specifically, but just think animated movies. Yeah, that one. He's a major film director.

We'd been living out in Atlanta. He was doing commercial work, but then he got offered this huge job and we left and came here. It'll be one of the world's largest movies. It'll be in all the theaters. You'll see posters for it at bus stops and ads before online videos. Your parents will encourage you to watch it. It will seem totally innocuous. But it will be more dangerous than any R-rated film.

We'll get to that in a bit.

IF YOU'RE INTO OLD PLACES, YOU'D SQUEAL IF YOU SAW MY neighborhood. Many of the homes were built in the 1930s, about a decade after the company my father works for started. Let's call it The Company. Anyway, these homes were built for many of the animators, so they could live close to the studios and zip on up to work every day without having to endure the total chaos that is Los Angeles traffic.

Which, by the way, occupies your mind and your life. Traffic, I mean. Like, your whole day can get completely ruined because you turned right instead of left. It could make you thirty minutes late, which will bump all your meetings, which will bump dinner, which will bump relaxing time, which will cause people like my dad to storm in, throw their things down at eleven at night, and drink themselves to sleep.

Basically, everyone here is pretty stressed out. Those who work at The Company, anyway. It makes me feel pretty isolated sometimes. Mom's not around much either. She works in real estate, and the market here is booming.

Which leaves me to hang out with myself. I've made a few friends, but what I really enjoy in Los Angeles is the library. Being a history nut, I decided a couple weeks ago to research the history of this neighborhood. There's a lot of information about its development, but almost none about my particular street. After digging through half a dozen books and browsing the Internet, I did find one source that actually mentioned my house. It was quite interesting.

It said that one of the original animators for The Company lived at my address. (Sorry, I can't give that to you. You might be creepy and strange, and even though I might not be here soon, and most of you wouldn't want to come anyway, *some* of you would, and only the complete psychos would really do it.) He had the house built specifically for him and his family, and it's as eccentric as he apparently was. First of all, it's two stories, but the top, where the attic is, is built like a citadel or something, so it ends in a point, like it's reaching straight up to the sky. Looks like a wizard's hat. And the shingles are all misshapen, on purpose, resembling a fantastical home. Same with the sides of the house. Even the door is slanted, purposefully. The whole place has a whimsical quality to it.

But it's also dark and strange, like an old movie you love because it's magical but also a bit creepy. Like it has the potential to be both good and bad, if such a thing exists.

There's all these nooks and crannies, too, that I didn't discover until recently. Like when I was rearranging my bedroom, sliding my dresser to the other side of the room, when I stumbled and knocked into the wall opposite my small walk-in closet. I wasn't sure I'd fit in the hole. Then my face got all hot, even though I was alone. I pulled my jacket tighter over my stomach. It was easier to hide from myself that way. Voices, in my brain. Calling me out for potentially being wider than the hole.

I shook my head. The voices left. That was good. They usually do if I just breathe and envision them cascading out of my mouth on each exhale.

::buries head in fat arms in total shame::

I went feet-first into the tunnel, shimmied my way until it turned downward, and lowered myself in, half-sitting, half-sliding until I hit bottom. Ahead of me, the tunnel looked like it opened up. I shifted my legs behind me and crawled a few feet until I entered a tiny room.

I shined my light to the left.

Sitting atop a ledge was a small child, eyes like dinner plates, with a strange grin, staring at me.

Chapter 2

Okay, it wasn't a child. But I thought it was, which is why I grabbed its arm and dragged it out of there.

After I'd climbed out of the tunnel and closed the secret door in my bedroom, I sat the wooden thing across from me on my dresser. Its head was smooth and shiny, with painted face and hair and clothes and hands. It had no movable joints, kind of like a marionette. Its eyes were wide, the lashes long, the smile tight-lipped. It was eerie and strange.

Yes, of course it was a boy.

And it looked a little . . . off. Not like a doll you'd buy in the store. It felt more like a prototype or something, like a proof of concept that animators or designers might create to show that a character "works." If you're confused, don't worry about it, it's just an industry thing.

And what was this tunnel that went nowhere inside my house? I checked the floor plans, the building history—every document we had—but I couldn't find any answers.

So I decided to sleuth some more.

In the bottom drawer of my parents' hideously massive file cabinet, I found one historical record that mattered: information about the first owners. In the 1920s, Bill B. was a character designer for The Company. Like many employees at these places, he's not mentioned in company documents, and the general public wouldn't have a clue who he was. Most entertainment jobs are like that. People are faceless, nameless, and the most talented ones, Dad says, never see anything close to fame.

Bill B. had a wife and two daughters. They lived here until 1946. After that, the house was sold to a few other families, which made us the fifth to live here.

I was still absorbed in the material when I heard the door open. I rubbed my eyes and looked at the time. 9:03 p.m. Quickly, I replaced the files and met Dad at the doorway.

Huge bags hung under his red eyes. He looked ridiculous, honestly, more like a cartoon character than a person. He sat and drank a beer. I took the opportunity to show him the doll. He set it on his lap, stared at it for a minute.

Then, his face brightened and his frown broke. "It's perfect," he said.

"For what?"

"One of the characters in the movie isn't going to work. But this little guy could be great."

I didn't think much of it at the time; I just shrugged and brought Dad his dinner, pleased that he seemed happier. And when I turned back from the hallway on my way to bed, he was holding the doll in his lap and was petting its shiny head, with an odd smile on his face.

CHAPTER 3

THUMP.

I opened my eyes. The neon numbers on the alarm clock read 3:16 a.m.

Thump.

Sitting up, I looked at my bedroom door. Listened closely. There it was—another *thump*. But not like something hitting against a wall. Something else.

I crawled out of bed, careful not to make the old floorboards creak, crouched on my hands and knees, and peeked under the door, where I could see a little glow from the night light shining down the hallway.

Thump. Thump. Thump.

A shadow passed under the door.

I froze. Why didn't I open it? Later I would yell at myself for that. I was too scared.

I was probably dreaming, I decided later.

There's no way that doll could have been walking down the hall.

THE NEXT MORNING, I EMERGED FROM MY BEDROOM IN time to see Dad off for work. He carried the doll under his arm and left. I felt better knowing it was out of the house.

Nothing weird happened after that, for the next couple nights at least. No strange thumps during the night. I even forgot about the door in the wall.

I went to school, tried to get to know other kids. They're nice enough, but I've always felt different from . . . well, everyone. Besides, I don't know about these L.A. girls. They're all so skinny. Also, by the time you're seventeen it seems harder to make new friends. I was always a bit of an introvert, and being the new girl doesn't help. I tried not to let it bother me and shoved the terrible voice in my head down, down, down somewhere dark and deep.

Alright, I admit it, I was lonely.

I got the courage to ask a girl in biology class, Melinda, to hang out after school. She was cool. She liked to climb in those indoor rock-climbing gyms, and she wore ripped jeans, which made me feel like she didn't care about fashion the way the others did. When the other girls wore ripped jeans, it was a fashion statement. But Melinda genuinely had no interest. I liked that.

We went to the mall in Burbank. It's kind of a consumerist hellhole, but there's a bookstore. Plus, it's air conditioned. We had fun trying on clothes and spying on boys in the food court. We played a game called "Who would you rather?" which is pretty self-explanatory. You just compare two boys and ask each other who'd you rather do bad things with. You have to explain why, of course, you can't just say this guy or that guy and not give a reason. It's fun to argue with each other.

Anyway, we were sitting there and something caught my attention. I hid, reflexively.

"What is it?" Melinda asked, sucking down a soda.

"My dad!"

"Huh?" She turned and watched him walk into a nearby hair salon. "Why are you hiding?"

Good question. I didn't know. It was instinctual, I guess. I wasn't sure what to tell her. For some reason it just felt right to hide.

He was walking funny, like he couldn't bend his legs at his knees too well. Also, there was something strange about his—

"Does his hair look weird to you?" I asked as I watched him through the storefront window.

Melinda squinted. "It looks like he buzzed one side or something."

"He didn't buzz it. He'd never do that. Wait, what's he buying?"

"Not sure." She smiled at me. That devious girl. "I'll check."

She hustled out of the food court, entered the salon, and pretended to study a shampoo bottle as the cashier rang up my dad. After he'd gotten his receipt, he left the mall. I turned away so he wouldn't see me.

Melinda puttered back, a confused look on her face. "He was buying spray-on hair."

"What?"

"Yeah. Like, uh, hair you spray on. He doesn't

normally use that, right? That stuff's gross."

"No. I don't think so. Mom likes to play with his hair. Or, she did."

"She's not gonna do that anymore." Melinda munched on a french fry.

I frowned. She was right about Mom. Even before this hair thing, my parents hadn't seemed to be getting along so well. Not since we'd moved. She was in Vegas for a real estate convention for the next week or so, so I couldn't joke with her about Dad's . . . spray-on hair? So bizarre.

Melinda burped, finishing her soda.

We had some more fun playing "F, Marry, Kill" while watching a new crop of boys stroll in, but the whole time I felt super uneasy, like I had seen my father doing something really bad, something he wouldn't want me or Mom to know about.

As it turns out, I was right.

CHAPTER 4

THE TICKING CLOCK READ 10:30 P.M. I'D FINISHED MY homework and taken a bath, and was carrying my plate of cheese and crackers into the living room so I could watch some horrible television alone.

Why are there so many shows about people who are famous for no reason? I've never understood it. We might as well be watching the life of a grocery store clerk. I'd watch that. Think of the nonsense they have to put up with. Customers demanding the chocolate-covered Twinkies that were discontinued years ago, for example.

Getting really angry about it, too. Screaming, spit flying from their red faces . . . Maybe that doesn't sound interesting to you. I guess rich people are fun to watch in their own way. I just prefer real people.

Still, I couldn't deny it would have been nice to be rich and famous. Life seems so easy for them. It doesn't matter if they "fit in" because everyone else is trying to fit in with *them*. They make the rules. That sounds *fantastic*.

The credits for some "Real Housewives" show had begun rolling when Dad walked in. It was dark in the entryway—just one dim bulb lit the door—but I could see he had what appeared to be a full head of hair.

It just looked a little shiny. Greasy.

::shudders in utter disgust::

He tossed his keys onto the small table next to the door. His movements looked stilted, jerky.

"Hey, Bunny," he said awkwardly.

He turned his entire upper half—from his waist—and stared at me straight on. I tried not to gasp when he stood in the light. Besides the spray-on hair on the right side of his head, there was—

"Dad, what's wrong with your eye?"

"Nothing. What's wrong with yours?" That was a dad joke.

"It looks like you got beat up." I stood. "Here, let me see—"

He yawned, waved me off, and hustled on stiff legs down the hall to the bedroom. "I'm beat, Lydia. Long day. Didn't even have lunch. We'll catch up tomorrow."

Boom. The door shut. And locked.

::stares dumbfoundedly at the wall for three-and-a-half minutes while contemplating Dad's flat, wooden-ass head::

I called my mom.

"Sorry, honey, I know I've been out of touch. I'll be back on Saturday. How's school?"

We talked for ten minutes. I felt sad. I wanted to tell her about Dad, but what was I supposed to say? *Hey Mom, Dad is using spray-on hair and he's looking weird and won't talk to me and I have one friend and isn't that cool and oh there's this doll and you have to come home right now because I'm freaked out but don't know why—*

I hung up and got ready for bed.

Maybe I'd feel better in the morning, I thought.

That's a laugh.

Little did I know, I'd feel much, much worse.

CHAPTER 5

THAT NIGHT. 2:47 A.M. A SCRATCHING SOUND RIPPED ME from my sleep.

::rolls over, half-awake, nearly loses her shit::

My father was crawling, belly-down, toward the secret door.

I watched his dim outline tap on the wall. The door opened. He half-crawled, half-wriggled into the hole, head-first.

The door gently shut behind him.

I must be dreaming.

But I wasn't.

My father had just slithered across my floor in the middle of the night and through a secret door in the wall.

I froze. Was it my father, or was it someone else?

It had to be him. Who else would come into my

house?

Who else even knew about the door?

Come to think about it, no one knew. Only I did.

And . . .

No.

The dummy knew about it.

But that's impossible, I told myself. The dummy wasn't *alive*. It couldn't see or think or hear, or even know that it had been taken out of its compartment.

Besides, what was I even saying? This was my *father*, not the doll. He must have known about the door in the wall and, and . . .

Nothing made any sense.

I set my feet down and tiptoed out of my room. I needed to check Dad's room and make sure he wasn't in there. If he wasn't, that meant he was in the tunnel. If he *was* in his room, then we for sure had some problems: namely, that someone else was in my house.

I pushed open his bedroom door.

His bed was empty.

So he really was down there.

What are you going to do now? Go back to bed, pretend to sleep, waiting and chattering your teeth, hoping to God or whatever might be out there that your dad hasn't lost his goddamn mind?

I decided to march into my bedroom, fling open that door, and yell: *What are you doing, Daaaaad?* I could even be annoying about it. Yeah, that's it. Be like a kid. The kid you are.

I stomped into my bedroom, strode to the back wall, flung open the secret door—

"Don't go down there."

I whipped around. Dad was sitting in my rocking chair, the one I'd had since I was four. Under any other circumstance his sitting in it might have been comical. But right now, I didn't see the humor.

Because the yellow night-light plugged into the outlet next to the rocking chair lit his face from underneath.

It looked like someone had taken a rough eraser to the right side of his dome. Little strands of hair clung to his skull like climbers on a cliff, but most of his head was just red, splotchy skin. He seemed to have no right cheekbone.

Like that side of his face was painted on.

"You don't want to go down there," he repeated. "It's not safe. I'm gonna seal it up." He motioned to the door in the wall. "I couldn't sleep. Figured it was a good time to check it out." He rubbed his temples. His voice was low, gravelly.

"Dad, your face—"

"Oh, that. I'll go to the doctor's. Maybe next week, we'll see."

"Can't you go tomorrow?"

He stood. "I'll get it done, don't worry."

He hugged me and then went to bed.

I froze.

If I hadn't felt what I felt, I'd have just thought I'd been making too big a deal about this whole thing. *Dad is having some weird health problem,* I'd have thought. *He was only going into that tunnel to check it out for himself. He couldn't sleep and thought that it might be a good time to do it. Fine.*

But here's the thing. He was wearing a ski jacket. Which was odd, but with everything else going on I hadn't given it much thought. Then we hugged, and I felt something beneath the layers of clothing.

And when he turned to leave, I caught a glimpse of

the thing underneath it.

The little arm.

The little *wooden* arm.

That was growing out of his side.

CHAPTER 6

YOU DON'T NEED ME TO TELL YOU IT IS NOT NORMAL FOR daughters to try and sneak a peek at their dads in the shower. There are just some things you don't want to know.

But how could I ignore what I'd felt and seen?

I felt the doll there. It was right against his skin. But how the hell could it be growing out of his side?

I know that my imagination can get a wee bit away from me. Like when I was four and thought I could fly. Didn't work out so well. My arm was in a cast for weeks.

Being alone most of the time doesn't help either. You get really weird when your only companions are YouTube or Snapchat personalities. It warps your mind. It has to. Like, you start seeing the real world through the filter of whatever you're feeding yourself.

And given that I listen to a lot of conspiracy and horror podcasts, I'm the first to admit it when my thinking gets wonky.

But I don't think that's what was happening.

I wanted to tell Melinda, but I didn't know her well enough just yet. Even if I had, I probably wouldn't want to admit something like this.

Something this strange.

Dad's behavior didn't help dissuade me, either. He

started leaving the house really early from then on. Like four or five in the morning. I didn't see him at all the next few days.

All of this added up to me wondering if I'd lost my freaking mind a little.

No. I knew something was definitely wrong. Even if Dad wasn't "merging" or whatever with the doll, what was he *really* doing in my room? His explanation just didn't make any sense.

Then it hit me.

He was searching for something.

But what?

LATER, AFTER CHASTISING MYSELF FOR THE FOUR COOKIES I snarfed down after school, I climbed down the tunnel behind the secret door and looked around. I found nothing.

When I got out, I moved my dresser back against the door. No more nightly trips for Dad. Also, I drilled a lock into my door frame. For privacy. Smart move, I told myself. I patted myself on the back a little.

I sat against the dresser and thought some more about what Dad was looking for.

What do you think he was looking for, dummy? He was looking for other dolls.

Hmm. That was an interesting thought. If there were other dolls in the house, but they weren't in my room, then there must be other hidden doors.

My body went cold. Jesus, were there really *more* of those things? If so, why were they hidden in our house?

Suddenly, I couldn't breathe. My vision swam. Everything was closing in on me. I trembled. I needed to get out.

Barefoot, I raced down the hallway and the stairs,

through the living room, flung open the door—

And screamed.

CHAPTER 7

"JESUS, WHAT'S WRONG WITH YOU?"

Melinda was standing there, clutching her school books to her chest, seriously concerned about this sweating crazy person with wild hair who just yelled in her face.

I gasped. "What are you doing here?"

She rolled her eyes. "Homework. At five. Remember?"

Oh, that.

I got red. "Sorry," I mumbled.

"What's wrong?"

"Nothing, I, uh . . ."

"Do you want to work inside?" She gestured to the house.

I froze. No, I didn't. I really didn't.

"Sure," I said anyway, then abruptly plopped onto my stoop and began to cry.

"WHAT DO YOU THINK?" I ASKED LATER AT THE KITCHEN table. "Am I crazy?"

It was dark out. The coffee Melinda had brought had gone cold long ago. She sipped it anyway, deep in thought.

"No, you're not crazy," she said. "Your dad *was* crawling through your room in the middle of the night. That's weird. You saw something wooden in his side.

That's weird, too. Plus, I saw him close-up at the mall. And he looked weird. It was really unsettling. I mean, maybe your dad isn't *becoming a doll*, but something for sure isn't right."

I could have hugged her.

"The question is," she said, draining the last of her coffee, "where should we start searching for the other dolls?"

That devious grin again.

This is a three-bedroom home. Two bedrooms and one-and-a-half baths on the top floor, and the master bedroom on the bottom.

The staircase to the second floor leads to an open balcony, so you can peer down onto the living room from above. It's cool. If I'd grown up here, I probably would have loaded the living room floor with cushy pillows and then leaped off the banister. I considered doing it now, but decided it was best to get our search done first.

There weren't many places for a secret door like the one in my room. We searched everywhere. Dad's office, all the bedrooms. I felt really weird crawling around the base of my parents' bed. The doodads and knick-knacks on their night stands were so personal. My snooping felt like a betrayal.

We were extra careful not to disturb anything. Dad couldn't know we'd been there. We moved desks and felt behind couches, knocking on the walls and gathering dust with our fingertips.

Melinda wiped the sweat from her forehead, leaving brown streaks. We'd been searching for almost an hour already, and we hadn't touched our biology books. *We do have a test tomorrow,* I reminded myself.

"We've gone through the entire house," she said, resting her back against the refrigerator.

"Yeah, guess so. What now?"

"Biology? Food?"

Yeah. Good idea. I tried to muster the energy to stand and grab a box of macaroni. Then I saw the cabinet above the fridge.

"Wait a second. Boost me up."

She helped me to my feet and interlocked her fingers. I stepped onto her hands and opened the cabinet. She didn't seem to strain under my weight, which made me feel good.

There was nothing inside.

Then I noticed the paneling in the back. It was darker than the rest of the interior. It looked out of place.

One knock from my fist and the secret door opened.

Melinda yelped in surprise as I sprang from her hands, propelling myself straight into the cupboard.

I gawked.

A tunnel inside, about six feet long. I crawled in, elbows slamming the sides. I could feel the slickness of blood on the metal walls. I'd be scabbed and bruised tomorrow, but I didn't care. I didn't think about it at all. My heart was beating so hard, I could feel it between my ears.

The tunnel twisted to the right. I pulled myself around the turn, on my side, and saw the thing sitting there.

MELINDA, POOR CREATURE, WAS STANDING IN FRONT OF the fridge, her hands over her mouth, when I tossed it down.

I can only imagine her surprise when out of this hole

in her new friend's strange house sprang a two-foot-tall little girl with jolly blonde curls and crooked, painted eyes.

CHAPTER 8

WE SAT IT UP ON THE KITCHEN TABLE. GOD, THIS NEW doll was creepy, and obviously from the same "family" as the other one.

Its face, features, and "clothing" were all painted on, just like the other one. And like the other doll, the wood was immaculately smooth. The body was stiff—no movable joints. And its expression? Bubbly and smiling.

A happy child with blonde curls. Definite charisma.

I guess.

We stared at it a while. This was supposed to be a big surprise, or so I thought. But now that we'd found it, the room deflated a bit.

"What are you going to do with it?" Melinda asked.

"I don't know. What *should* I do? I don't want to give it to Dad. He's already obsessed with one doll. He said the other day the studio loves it; they're revising the entire family in the movie now."

"That's cool, right? I mean, that your dad is a big-time director. And you're influencing the project. That's a good thing."

I shifted in my seat. She had a point. But it didn't do much for our current situation.

So I made us some mac and cheese. When I brought it to the table, Melinda was staring at the doll. Later, I'd think of a better word to describe her look. The word was "smitten."

"I guess you're going to put it back up there?" she asked, flicking her head at the cabinet above the fridge.

I shrugged and ate the half-cup of food I'd allowed myself. "Got any better ideas?"

"I could take it home with me."

I looked sideways at her.

"That way you can keep it out of the house and your dad won't find it." She looked down at her glop. "At least, until you figure something else out."

Maybe I should have said no. But I was so creeped out. I'd feel a lot better knowing it was out of the house.

So I let her take it.

But I shouldn't have.

::hangs head in everlasting shame::

It was past midnight and I was in bed when I heard the front door open. Footsteps moved down the hall. I waited until the water pipes had stopped squealing (which meant Dad had finished showering), then gave it another hour to make sure he was really asleep.

I tiptoed onto the landing and down the stairs. Dad's office is down the hallway on the bottom floor, opposite his bedroom. I paused near his door and waited until I heard him snoring.

Good. I was all set.

Gently closing the office door behind me, I flicked the light on, took the blanket off my dad's reading chair, and shoved it under the door frame. That should cut any telltale light coming under the door.

He'd left his briefcase on the desk. Just like I'd hoped.

I love his briefcase. It's red and old-school, and he looks like a weirdo when he carries it around.

I popped it open.

A binder of storyboards. Another one with legal documents. All neatly maintained.

At the bottom was a manila folder. I opened it. It contained old, faded news clippings from the 1930s. I sat back in the office chair and began reading.

"The Company Shuts Down Newly Formed Animation Department," the headline said. Beneath that was the story, only a couple paragraphs long.

On Tuesday, The Company abruptly announced it will be canceling its work on the upcoming film, See You in Theaters. *Insiders say The Company will take a massive loss on abandoning the project, currently in pre-production. The department heads have made no comments.*

Bill B. has stepped down, announcing an early retirement: a surprising move for the forty-four-year-old lead animator. He has also refused to comment, though one anonymous source told us he and the studio suffered from "creative differences," the project being "too dark" for The Company's new president.

Too dark? What did that mean?

I removed the storyboards from their plastic sheaths.

They gave me pause.

The drawings were nasty. I stared with creeping flesh at the contorted faces, the long teeth, the twisted smiles. This was like no kids' film I'd ever seen.

I turned the page. Six frames depicted a small girl, tied to a chair, while an adult wearing a doctor's smock and surgical mask towered over her with what looked like a giant metal claw; its sharp fingers spun around in whip-fast motion, like an electric kitchen mixer. Or a weed trimmer.

It was torture, pure and simple.

The storyboards didn't show the gore explicitly; the

film would cut to another small girl standing in the corner, obviously gleeful at the display of carnage. The viewer would hear the sounds of torture, but never see the torture itself.

I slammed the book shut.

The girl in the corner looked just like the doll we'd found earlier.

THE NEXT MORNING, I RACED TO SCHOOL AND WAITED BY Melinda's locker. The warning bell rang; she still hadn't shown. Disappointed, I went to class, figuring she'd slept in. I'd see her in biology.

But she wasn't there, either. It wasn't like her to miss class, and especially not when we had a huge test that counted for twenty percent of our grade. I asked Mr. Kemp if she'd called in sick, but he said no.

I texted. I called. It went straight to voicemail.

The next day, she didn't show up again.

KNOCK, KNOCK.

I stood at her front door, waiting, hands in the pockets of my loose-fitting jacket, feeling very awkward. Melinda lived all the way in Beverly Hills, even though she went to school on the East Side. And her neighborhood was uber wealthy; her house was the only one on the block without a gate.

I shouldn't be here. Leave. Forget we were ever friends and just go. She doesn't like me. I was stupid to think she would. She's cute and rich and thin and people like her.

I shook my head, took a few deep breaths like my therapist in Atlanta had told me to do. No sense in thinking like that, I told myself.

I rang the doorbell twice more. Still no answer. Frustrated, I slammed my hand down on the door handle. To my surprise, the door opened, revealing an immaculate, white entryway with twenty-five-foot ceilings. A large staircase jutted out of the center of the room and stretched to the second floor, where the walkway and banisters wrapped around the sides of the interior. For a moment, I forgot all about why I was there and just marveled at the statues and framed portraits of nude women.

"Melinda?" I called, gently. My voice echoed. I tried again.

Then—

A door creaked. I heard footsteps. Up on the second floor.

I called again and stepped inside. I walked up the stairs and pushed open the first door to the left. Band posters littered the walls. Clothing was strewn around. This was her room, all right. She had her own bathroom in there, too.

I knocked on the closed bathroom door. "Melinda?"

"Go away," she said in a muffled voice. Sounded like she was crying. With her hands over her face. "Just go away."

I put my ear to the door. First she hadn't come to school, then didn't answer my calls, now this.

I felt a sudden wave of sadness. I'd just found Melinda. She was my first friend in so long, and now she was telling me to leave. Mom and Dad were both basically absent. Did I have no one left?

I leaned in. I spoke loudly and clearly and slowly, so she could hear me, really *hear* me. She needed to understand. I told her that whatever was going on, it was safe to tell me. I wouldn't reject her, or think she was weird, or tell anyone if something had happened. I needed her, I told her, I needed her to let me in, to talk to her. I wiped the tears from my eyes.

I heard the click of the lock.

The handle turned. The door opened.

I saw the rest in fragments:

—Steam billowing out.

—Melinda's face, makeup streaming down.

—Her shoulder.

—And the second head attached to it.

Not just a head, though.

A frame. A frame of a body.

Oh, no—

And two tiny arms.

Melinda sniveled and looked at the doll that was attached to her. "Get it out of me."

I gawked, aghast.

The doll was sticking out of her left shoulder, cut off at the chest at a forty-five-degree diagonal. The right arm was submerged up to the elbow near her collarbone, as if it had been swallowed up while flailing at sea.

I couldn't tell where she ended and it began. There was no blood. They'd been fused seamlessly. The wood from the doll and the skin from my friend were overlapping, the resulting area looking like the skin of a burn victim, stretched and horribly painful-looking.

"Get it out," she repeated, sobbing.

I placed my hands under the doll's wooden arms and pulled.

And pulled some more.

And yanked.

But it wouldn't budge. It was like trying to pull a table apart with my bare hands.

I shook my head. It was no use.

The doll was hopelessly stuck inside her.

CHAPTER 9

IT TOOK TWO HOURS TO CALM MELINDA DOWN.

"Here." I handed her a cup of tea. Decaf, Jesus Christ, decaf.

"Thanks," she said, glancing at the blanket we had thrown over the doll. She frowned and quickly looked away.

Now, try to picture how creepy and awkward this situation would be if you were me. You're with a new friend you kind of know but not really, and somehow a *doll* is stuck halfway out of her body. What do you say that isn't wildly dumb or insensitive?

Also, it felt like I'd just caught her naked or something. It felt very revealing. Not sure how else to describe it.

"I'm screwed." Her eyes glazed over. Her look said it all. Nowhere to go, nothing she could do.

Still, I tried to reason things out. "Okay, first things first. Are your parents coming home soon?"

She shook her head. "They're gone on a business trip. Four or five days, I think."

I paced her bedroom, trying to make it look like I had a plan, or was at least capable of formulating one. "We need to get this thing out of you. That's the most important thing. I'll take you to the hospital."

"So you can pawn me off on them? So they can keep me there, locked down, like some kind of freak prisoner? When they see that a *doll* is sticking out of me, they'll flip out. They'll call in the army or something. That's what always happens in the movies. They'll want to do tests on me! They'll cut me open!"

I saw her point. That did seem to happen a lot in movies. I decided to change tactics. Maybe we could come up with some answers on our own. "Okay. So how did this happen?"

She stared into her mug. "I came home with it from your place. There was something . . . attractive about it, I guess. I'm not sure what drew me to it.

"When I got here I put it on my chair, just kind of forgot about it. I was so fried, I climbed into bed and went to sleep. But when I woke up the next morning . . ." She looked forlornly at the blanketed mass on her shoulder. "It was lying next to me."

"You didn't put it in bed with you?"

"No way!"

"What happened the next night?"

She shook her head. "I don't know. I felt so weird and tired. I stayed home from school and slept. Like, all day. I only got up to use the bathroom, once, and I got some water. Other than that, I slept straight through the day and night.

"I woke up this morning, and before I opened my eyes I knew was having more trouble lifting my arm. It felt . . . heavy. Then I looked over and saw this." She motioned to the bulk attached to her and spouted fresh tears.

I felt terrible. But I also knew one of us needed to stay strong. I had to figure this out.

"It attaches itself to you when you sleep," I concluded, half to her and half to myself.

She nodded, wiping her face. "I think so."

"And you woke up this morning, and it's been the same since?"

"Yes."

I nodded. "Okay. At least we know how to stop it from getting worse."

"But what am I supposed to do? I have to sleep!"

"Not until we figure this out," I said bluntly.

She threw up her hands. "And how do we do that?"

I pulled out my binder. "I took the storyboards out of Dad's briefcase before he left for work yesterday. I made some copies." I flipped it open. "I found notes about the production, too. This movie that was *supposed* to be made back in the day was horrific, way too violent for kids. The studios picked it up originally to compete overseas with German films."

"Germany?"

"Yeah. During the 1920s and 30s, Germany was producing these animations. Weird stuff. They were dark and strange, popular in some circles, but The Company thought they could market similar movies to the American audiences. So they hired Bill B. and gave him a project. This project."

I flipped through the binder. "The story's about a 'normal' family living in America, except that they're not normal at all. And that's where it gets really creepy."

She pointed to a frame in the book. "That's the doll! What's she doing?"

"She's burrowing inside the little girl of the family."

"Oh." She sat back.

I showed her another storyboard.

"That's a swastika!" she exclaimed.

I nodded.

"Why would they put a swastika in the movie?"

"Back in the 1930s," I explained, "things were rough for America and Europe. The Depression was on. Things looked pretty bleak. And the Nazi party was picking up steam at the time. Tapping into the anger and frustration of many people around the world. Lots of people don't know this, but we had a huge Nazi party in America during the 1930s."

"Really?"

"Yeah. It wasn't as big a deal as you might think. The Nazis hadn't murdered millions of people yet. And the president of The Company, he thought he could tap into that market, and even convert some people. To the Nazi party."

"Why the hell would anyone do that?"

"Because he was a Nazi too."

"Oh."

I continued. "As the story goes—as far as I can tell—this normal family was living in an average place. But they weren't normal. They'd . . . burrow into people. Take over their brains. Make them do things. They were bent on world domination. Said they were the one true kind of human. The master race. Or the next stage in evolution, maybe. I'm not entirely sure. That's just what I've been able to gather."

"This family. How big is it?"

"I only have a few of the original storyboards, but I see three people: the dad, the mom, and—" I gestured to the doll.

"So this thing is taking me over? Is that what's happening?"

I deflated a bit. "I think so. It seems to be doing to you what that other one's doing to my dad."

She wiped away her tears and took a deep breath. She appeared more determined. "Will you do me a favor?" she asked.

"Of course. Anything."

"Cut this goddamn thing out of me."

CHAPTER 10

"I CAN'T DO THIS." THE ELECTRIC SAW QUIVERED IN MY hand. Melinda was face-up on the work table. We'd pulled the top half of the doll as far away from her body as we could, which wasn't much.

"Of course you can. Just cut the head off."

Pause. I shook my head.

"Come on! I trust you."

I wasn't sure. I had a bad feeling. But Melinda kept refusing to go to the hospital. Besides the first point she'd made earlier, what if the first thing the doctors did before cutting it out was put her to sleep?

No, she'd said, we're doing this ourselves.

She was right. We couldn't have her put to sleep.

I looked at the saw in my hand. I'd never used one before. Could I do this?

What choice did I have?

I nodded at her. Okay.

If you'd walked in on us right then, you'd have been convinced that either a deranged surgeon or a serial killer was about to do something very nasty to a poor, defenseless little girl . . .

And half a wooden body.

God, this was weird.

I plugged the saw in, flicked the "On" switch. The blade whirred to life. It was *loud*.

Melinda squeezed her eyes shut and turned away, grimacing.

I bent my legs, got into a wide stance. I had to be sure I didn't accidentally drop the thing. *Two hands now, kiddo.*

Lowered the blade. Melinda squeezed her eyes shut

harder.

Lower.

I touched the surface of the doll's neck, just below the chin.

I've never heard a scream like that before.

I yanked the saw away, turned it off, and let it drop. Tears were streaming down Melinda's face. The sobbing. I felt so bad.

The saw had only cut about half an inch deep into the wood. It was black down there below the smooth surface and the paint. Tendrils of smoke floated up from the wound.

She clutched the doll with her right hand, as if the skin I'd cut were her own.

"Water!" she sobbed.

I ran inside, grabbed a glass, filled it, and rushed back. Poured it on the wound. It sizzled, made her scream louder. She reached a shaking hand up to the doll's head.

Eventually, she was able to get up off the table.

Eventually.

LATER, I SAT IN THE BATHROOM, WRAPPING THE WOUND with gauze.

"That's what it feels like," she said, popping three extra-strength Advil. "Like it's *my* skin and bone. It hurts like you just buried a saw into *my* neck."

We stared at each other as if we'd just hiked through twenty-seven miles of desert at high noon. She smiled. I took her hand.

"What now?" I asked.

"Will you help me stay awake? We have to figure this out."

I said of course, but I had no clue what to do next.

And night was falling.

CHAPTER 11

WE DECIDED TO STAY AT MY HOUSE. MAYBE THERE WAS some clue we were missing that would help us solve this thing. The trick would be hiding her from Dad. Didn't need him getting involved.

Driving to my house took longer than expected. Los Angeles traffic is singularly torturous between the hours of 5 p.m. and 8 p.m. And also between 8 p.m. and midnight. And sometimes between midnight and 5 p.m.

I drove with the air conditioning blasting, windows down, trying to keep Melinda alert. She cracked open another energy drink, downed half of it. We must have looked like deranged triplets, the three of us in a row across the front seats.

At least I'd made a friend.

Or two.

::shivers, drools::

"I just thought of something," Melinda said, handing me the rest of her drink.

"What?"

"The storyboards say there were three members of the family, right?"

"Yeah."

"That means there's still one more doll somewhere."

How had we not thought about that?

Ah, God.

Please, no more.

FORTUNATELY DAD WASN'T HOME, SO GETTING MELINDA inside was relatively painless, though she did accidentally crack her new wooden head on the doorframe coming in, which she said felt just like slamming her own head. I would have thought this whole situation utterly ridiculous, but it's hard to take these things lightly when you're directly involved.

I cleaned out space in my closet. We figured it would be best if she had a place to hide when Dad came home, until he went to bed. What would he think if he saw a wooden head springing from my friend's shoulder?

Would he be shocked? Or delighted?

My thoughts swarmed. *Do I try to save Dad, or Melinda? How do I even save Melinda? I have no plan. I'm hungry. Really hungry. There's no time for food. Yes, there is. Keep cleaning. Shut up, brain.*

And so on.

Finally, I finished cleaning. We ate. The clock read 8:06 p.m. Dad wasn't getting home these days until past ten or eleven.

"Something about taking them out of their spots triggered them to life," she said when we were all set up. "It's when all this started, right? Do the storyboards mention that?"

"It doesn't. We do know, though, that they're trying to get into our bodies while we sleep. And it has something to do with these old movies."

"What do you think it wants with me?" she asked. "What happens when it takes you over completely?"

Pause. That, I didn't want to think about.

Just then—

Boom.

"Lydia, you home?"

I heard   the clank-slide of keys tossed onto the

kitchen table.

"Hey." I bounced down the stairs, trying to appear chipper. I turned the corner toward the kitchen and skidded to a stop. "Dad?"

Deep, pockmarked rivers ran through his cheeks, accentuating the natural curves in his face. Dark brown rings hung under his eyes. His hair was sparser than before, his face even flatter.

He looked exactly the way I'd picture him if he'd been possessed by a wooden doll. A perfect composite of the two of them.

I quickly tried to hide my horror, to play it off. *Oh, nothing's wrong, Dad. It's not like I suspect you're merging with an old creepy doll made by a Nazi.*

That thought made me realize something else:

If it had taken over Dad's body, what was it doing to his mind?

He frowned. I felt like he was reading my thoughts. He knew. Somehow, he knew.

I smiled a little too wide. "How's the movie going, Dad?"

"Fine." He loosened his tie and plunked a paper bag down on the table. "Things are moving along nicely." He pulled a bottle of Scotch from the bag and poured a glass.

"I have a question for you." He sat down, crossing his legs. "The doll you found. Did you find any others?"

I shook my head.

"Hmm. Too bad."

"Are there more or something?"

"Three more. Four total."

"Four?" I tried to seem curious, but not overly so. We'd thought there were only three. What was this fourth one?

"Mmm." He took a long drink. "A father, a mother, two children. Both daughters."

"Maybe you'll find them," I offered.

"I've looked. Come here, I want to show you something."

He rose from his chair. "See that?" He opened the cabinet above the fridge, the one we'd found the other doll behind. Pushing the false wall in, he exposed the tunnel. "Just like the one in your room. Only, there's nothing in there." He let the wall fall; it banged loudly, making me jump. "Know anything about that?"

My father had never laid a finger on me. He'd been like the perfect dad. But seeing him towering over me like that, his face haggard, in some kind of permanent scowl, his skin all taut and ragged, I began to shake. I tried to hide it, really I did, and I almost got away with it, except—

He gripped my shoulders. I looked at his hands and nearly started crying. They had turned almost black. Skin was flaking off in large chunks. His fingernails were long and yellow.

I pretended not to notice.

He stared down on me with big yellow eyes. Veins crisscrossed in the white parts. They weren't his eyes. They looked painted on. "Did you take the doll from that tunnel?" he asked.

"No." I barely croaked it out. *God, take me anywhere but here.* I needed to pee. I needed to run. I'd never felt those two things so badly before in my life.

He frowned again but turned away. His claw-hands fell from my shoulders. He looked so tired, like he was having trouble keeping his arms up. "It's important that I find the rest of them. Very important."

I looked past him, to the dinner table. Several boxes

of files.

"Old archives," he said, then plopped down again. I turned away and began to tiptoe back upstairs, when—

"You're going to be very famous soon, Lydia. Did you know that? Very famous."

I stopped. "Huh?"

"You heard me. Famous beyond your wildest dreams. Bigger than those Instagram stars you love, bigger than the YouTubers, all of them."

"What do you mean? Those people have millions of followers. I don't even *have* a YouTube account—"

"Doesn't matter. You will. If you want. Like your mom."

"Mom? What does she—"

He waved a hand, dismissing my question. "You know I've always wanted the best for you, yeah? Here's my chance. My movie. You'll see."

"How is your movie going to make me and Mom famous?"

He smirked. "Because you're going to be in it, too. We all are. One big family that America will love."

Erm . . .

He continued. "Those billboards you see everywhere, the giant posters lining the corner of Hillhurst and Sunset. Can you picture your faces on them? Wouldn't that be unbelievable? For millions of young girls—and boys, ooh la la—to be obsessed with you? You'd never have to work, never have to go to college if you don't want to—and if you did, you could go *anywhere* you wanted.

"One of the best parts about being famous—I've been told—is that you never have to worry about money again. You have to take care of your money, of course, but if you had longevity in the business you could basically do whatever you wanted, knowing that there's always another job right around the corner.

"Then the question is, how do you become so popular that you become relevant and stay that way? You need a message, something that resonates with the people. An idea—yes, that's it! An idea that can stand the test of time. An idea that maybe the people don't even quite know they need to hear. And when they hear it, they can't resist it. It lodges in their mind and grows and grows, until they can't dig it out and don't even want to. In fact, they don't even realize it's there.

"It's got to hit on a solid, emotional level. It has to be a truth that you can't deny to your innermost self. Something people know they want but cannot touch, wouldn't even think to touch. Until you give it to them. Until you give them permission to touch it.

"There's only one thing people want, Lydia. People say they want to be happy, or have a purpose, or a career, or a family. I believe them, to an extent. But trust me, what they want is something deeper."

He leaned in. "People want *power*, Lydia. They want power over their surroundings, their bodies, other people. Don't believe me? Look at any celebrity. They want others to see them, to want to *be them*. That's power."

He took a long drink. "Look at the world today. We live in factions. It's all about the tribe, not the truth. People you admire, that's who create facts. Doesn't matter if you rape or kill, so long as you're on the right team. What do you think war is all about? What has it *ever been about*? It's about dominating the other—the same way a person maintains power over another, bending them to their will—so that when you commit violence against them, it's sanctioned. Very ordinary, very acceptable.

"Listen, honey, I know I'm rambling. You're young and may not understand all these things, but look at your own experience. Think about school. None of the groups let you in, do they? Not in New York, not in Atlanta, not here. You know why? Because they're off getting liked and you're not. You're not one of the tribe. Not yet.

"We can change that now." He knew he had my attention. "But only with the dolls. None of this works without all four of the dolls, do you understand?"

I stood there a long time.

Dad finished his drink, then grabbed his bottle and a few papers and stood.

"If you find another," he said, patting me on the shoulder as he left the kitchen, "let me know."

I felt a lump in my throat. I couldn't respond. I nodded.

Satisfied, he went to his office.

CHAPTER 12

A FEW MINUTES LATER, I LAID MY HEAD AGAINST MY bedroom door. I needed a breather.

Whatever Dad believed, well, he was damn serious about it.

Where did that talk about celebrities come from?

And what was the doll doing to his brain?

I entered my room, shut the door, and went to the closet. "Melinda," I said, moving aside the boxes I'd stacked in front of her, "we have to find the other dolls before—"

No!

I hurled everything aside and shook my sleeping friend awake, scream-whispering, "Melinda! Wake up, wake up!"

"Huh?" She rolled her head, opened her eyes groggily. "How long have I been out?"

I tore the blanket off her shoulder and gasped.

The doll had dug deeper. Only the top half of its head was sticking out now, from its nose on up. It stared, as if challenging me.

Almost too late.

I'll get her when she sleeps, I could feel it say.

Los Angeles never gets truly dark. Not even in the suburbs, twenty, thirty miles east. And definitely not in my neighborhood. It must be the smog. It kind of hangs over the city, trapping light and moisture. If you stayed in the city your entire life, you'd probably see, like, three stars. It turns the environment into a kind of bubble. It traps you.

I've heard the same thing said about the city itself.

I waited by my window, watching the scrappy trees sway in the wind. I was waiting for true night—at least, as much as the city would allow.

Melinda sat in the closet. Music played softly from my laptop, which I'd set by the door. Not so loud that I couldn't hear Dad coming up the stairs but not so soft that he could hear me talking quietly to Melinda.

"I can't hold out much longer." Melinda was struggling to keep her eyes open.

"Here." I fed her two more caffeine pills. Extra strength.

I popped two more, too, though I wasn't sure I needed them. The terror I felt was enough to keep me awake.

"There's gotta be something we missed," I said. I was sitting on my purple inflatable chair. I realized I was running my hands through my hair, pulling at the roots while I thought. *Ow. Ease up a bit, sweetness, no sense in going bald over this.* "A hiding spot, somewhere. And we have to find it before Dad does."

"No, we don't." Melinda was pacing around my room, trying to keep her back straight, arms stretched out, keeping blood flowing. The ridiculous half-head bobbed with her shoulders. "If we find it and take it out of whatever hole it crawled into, it's going to come alive and get us. Us meaning you, girl." She shook her head. "It's already got me."

She swayed a little. Woozy. I had to fight the urge to ask if she thought it was taking over her mind. So far, though, she seemed normal. She didn't seem to want to talk about it.

It reminded me of why I liked her so much. What drew me to her in the first place. Even though she was wealthy, she'd had a tough life. Her parents were basically absent. Her real father, her biological father, had left when she was a year old. She'd never known him. When her mother remarried, she and Melinda's new stepfather had started taking long, expensive vacations, leaving Melinda at home.

And even though she'd had everything handed to her—some would call her an overly privileged white girl—there was a sadness behind her eyes that I understood.

"But if we don't find it," I argued, "then Dad *will.*" I looked up. "We have to destroy it. Smash it at a junkyard. Burn it to a crisp, scatter the ashes. Anything. Dad said that he needs all of the dolls for his plan to work. Maybe that means if we destroy one of them, they all lose their power. Maybe this all goes back to normal."

"I don't want to find another one of those things."

"Neither do I." I looked at her. "But what choice do we have?"

For the next fifteen, twenty minutes I scoured the papers in the folders we had. But I found nothing.

I threw the papers aside and stood up. I paced around, my face growing red, my voice starting to shake. I wanted to give up.

Melinda calmly sat in my place, studied the next page for a moment. "What's this?"

I craned my head over her shoulder. She was pointing at a diagram of the back yard. There was a box with measurements on the sides: 8' and 10'.

"A shed, maybe?" I said. "But there's nothing in my backyard. It's just grass and some trees."

"Look here." Melinda's finger traced the page. "This wasn't just a shed. See?" She flipped to more detailed sketches. "It looks like a fallout shelter or something."

Hmm. I hadn't thought of that.

"So, this structure would be . . ." I went to my bedroom window overlooking the backyard and pointed. "Right there?"

Melinda joined me, drawings in hand. She squinted. "Yeah, the upper-right part of the yard."

I frowned. I couldn't see a thing. Maybe it was never built. Maybe these were just plans and nothing more.

Boy, was I wrong.

CHAPTER 13

AT 3:48 A.M. WE CREPT THROUGH THE KITCHEN AND INTO the back yard, careful to slide the back door open ever so gently. Every time it scraped against the bottom railing, my heart leapt. Melinda and I pushed up on the door handle to release some of the friction. Dad was asleep down the hall, and probably couldn't hear us, but who knows how well half-doll men really hear, *amiright?*

We crossed the back yard, feeling vulnerable and naked in the diffused light of the never-dark sky. It suddenly felt eerie, like all the plants and trees were watching us. Were they with us, or against us? I like to think they were cheering for us, those decades-old trees who had possibly even been around when the house was built, who knew all its secrets and were waiting with eager amusement to see if we too would discover them.

Grab the popcorn, I told them mentally. *I'm glad we could put on a show for you this evening. To my right is the magnificent shaking Melinda. Don't let her clutching my arm fool you. She's tough as stone and could kick your ass, even with half a doll head poking out of her.*

We reached the spot. Melinda made a rough outline in the grass with her shovel, showing me where the shed was supposed to be. We gently pressed our shovels into the rocky ground and stood on the edges. Quietly, we began removing the grass and dirt and piling it along the back fence.

About three inches down, our shovels struck something hard. We knelt down and swept the dirt away until the boarded-up entrance made of plywood was revealed.

I studied the edges. The wood was nailed down. I

jammed the claw end of a hammer underneath the plywood, braced myself with bent knees, then stood up.

The plywood came up easily. Decades of weather had weakened the nails. We set it aside.

I clicked the flashlight on my phone. A bright beam lit up a short stairwell walled with wood. Little rocks fell into the hole. I began the descent.

When I reached the bottom, I shined my flashlight around. It was dark, damp, dingy. The floor was dirt; the walls were just wood with huge swaths of insulation stuck between the beams. It didn't look like any kind of bomb shelter I'd ever seen in the movies.

"Hey," Melinda whispered. She was hunkered down on the other side of the room, pointing at something in the wall. I squinted as I approached.

The wooden slats that made up that portion of the wall ended about two feet from the floor. Underneath them was a blank piece of wood, square in shape.

Melinda knocked on it. Nothing. She shrugged and stood up.

"Wait." I handed her the light, knelt down, and tapped gently on the wood. *Thunk, thunk.*

Bracing myself on the floor like a catcher, I placed both hands on the piece of wood and slid it to the left, revealing—

"A tunnel?" I looked up at Melinda in confusion.

She backed away. Her light wavered.

I simply nodded at her and began crawling.

I wasn't as claustrophobic as I thought I'd be. Maybe it was because I'd done this before and was used to it, or maybe it was because I knew I had to be strong for Melinda. Either way, I crawled fast through that tunnel until I reached another wall, maybe eight feet in. This wall was made of wood, too. With one push it gave way, and I rolled headfirst into a larger area.

Bones were chained to the walls. Once complete skeletons, the ligaments had broken down over time, leaving only bits and pieces in the spots anchored by metal. Six bodies. Fully decayed. At some point, animals had gotten into this crypt. Some of them had died too, as the rat skeletons on the ground attested.

I stood in shock, growing dizzy. I stumbled back, tripped, fell to the ground. My phone skittered across the dirt. Crawling hastily, I snatched it up, whirled around on my knees—

And came face to face with another doll.

My skin grew ice cold. I began to shake. I choked on my own inhale.

I swallowed hard, then held my light up to the doll's face. It belonged to the same family as the others, that was for sure. Same flat features, though this one was decidedly skinny. A gaunt face, long eyelashes, and pursed lips. Representing a girl about my age, it had a model-esque quality to it. Of everyone I'd seen in the little demented family, I assumed this girl was the one most likely to be a star.

Upon seeing it, and holding it in my hands, I felt a strange sympathy. An instant bond of some kind, though it's difficult to explain. Sort of how you feel when you find an old toy you had growing up, one that you thought was lost long ago, but upon finding it buried in your closet a whole flood of emotions and memories pours into you, and you remember what it felt like to be a child.

I blinked, snapping myself back to reality. *You're in a room of death,* I told myself, and I turned to leave.

Melinda shouldn't have been waiting in the makeshift doorway. But she was, mouth open, staring at the room of bones.

"Come on," I whispered. She crawled back down the hall. I followed, sliding the wooden door shut behind us. When we reached the main room and felt the breeze, my legs suddenly gave out. I sank to the earth, dropped the doll, and just sat there. Exhausted, I looked up through the entrance at the diffused sky.

Melinda sat down in front of me, grabbed my head, and forced me to look at her. "Listen. Are you okay?" I nodded. "Good," she said. "Let me take over. Here's what we're going to do . . ."

Bless that girl. I was toast, for the moment anyway, and needed time to get my head on straight. She laid out a plan. We'd drive to the mountains, somewhere off the 210, in the Los Angeles Crest Mountains, and burn the doll. It sounded simple enough.

Time to move.

As I stood, a dark shadow interrupted the moonlight. I looked up, but there wasn't enough time to glimpse the face. Then there was nothing, because the trap door slammed shut.

I ran up the steps and pounded on the door, but then I heard the electric drill, and the screws being ratcheted into place, and I knew we were sealed in.

Chapter 14

I'd never been trapped in the dark before. Like, the real dark. Pitch black, I mean. Once I was on a school field trip and a guide took us into a cave, and I couldn't see my hand in front of my face. That was real dark. Like now.

It took a few minutes for Melinda and me to get our bearings down there. I grabbed and pulled her close, and I didn't even notice the little friend who was still attached to her shoulder. We screamed until our voices were hoarse. We decided no one could hear us. Better to save our strength.

We tried to be rational. It had to be Dad who trapped us. Whatever had taken him over—that character—was in charge now.

A couple hours passed. The heat down there was slowly cooking us. Soon we were stripped to our underwear. I'm glad she can't see me, I thought, then felt ashamed at thinking that.

I DID SOME QUICK CALCULATIONS. I FIGURED IT HAD BEEN five or six hours since I'd had any water. Not good. Sweating would soon dehydrate me. Food was less of an issue; I was too amped up to eat, anyway. I figured I had a handful of hours before liquids would be a real problem, so I set my mind to figuring out how to escape.

Melinda, though, had other issues. When the heat settled down on her, she got lethargic. Which meant she was sleepy. Not good. We had to find a way out, and fast.

I scoured the back room for an exit. I ran my hand over the walls. They were made of plywood, which, if we'd had tools, might not have presented a problem. But I didn't have anything to use.

I crawled to the back room. With an icky feeling, I tore one of the leg bones off a skeleton with a couple of yanks and twists. Maybe it would work as a makeshift shovel. I tore another off and handed it to Melinda. Hopefully the hard labor would keep her awake long enough to get out of here.

But nothing worked. After an hour, we gave up. We had no leverage coming at the wood from below. We really needed a crowbar. I thought about using another bone to shave mine down until we had a flat edge, but bone on bone simply didn't work like that.

Melinda collapsed next to the ladder. "How much time until we run out of air, you think?" she asked. I didn't answer. I just held her, and pretty soon our panting softened.

Gently, to my shame, we drifted to sleep.

Chapter 15

I jerked awake and sat up, rubbing the dirt from my face. "Melinda?" I whispered into the dark. "Melinda!"

No answer. With a sinking feeling, I shined my flashlight around the outer room. She wasn't there. The door to the inner room was shut.

I turned to my right. And screamed. Because the doll, the one we'd found down here, was sitting just two feet away, its arms outstretched toward me.

Shoving it away, I rolled onto my stomach and crawled to the opposite side of the room. I settled, holding the beam of my flashlight on it, waiting for it to move.

It didn't move.

After my heart settled, I checked my watch. I'd only been asleep for fifteen minutes. Not enough time for it to get me. I trembled at the thought.

But, Melinda.

I called to her again. Still no answer. I went to the

inner door and was about to set my hand on the knob, when it turned on its own.

I backed away. The door creaked open. My flashlight beam wavered. Soon I felt the other wall against my back, and Melinda crawled through the door in front of me and stood.

Her hair was curly blonde now instead of brown. Like Dad's, her face was flatter, and glowed like wood stained with expensive lacquer. Her nose had completely receded into her face. It looked more like a drawing of a nose.

I tracked my light down her body. Her waist had been sucked in, like she'd worn a corset for years. The changes seemed to be more intense on the right side, almost as if they were a wave washing over her.

Whatever she was, she was not Melinda anymore. She was becoming that *thing*, that character from the storyboards.

We didn't move, just stared at each other. Was she stuck halfway between doll and girl? Was the woman inside her still reeling in her new body?

She smiled a creepy-friendly smile.

Boom. Boom. Boom.

Up above.

Someone. Up there.

A shovel. Carving into the dirt.

Yes, it had to be. I could hear the crunching clearly.

Who was it? Was Dad digging us out?

Then, a shout. I could hear my name. Was I dreaming it? No.

I climbed the ladder and hurled myself against the plywood, banging with my fist. "Mom! Mom, let me out!"

"Hang on!" she half-yelled, half-whispered, frantically digging more dirt.

I could have cried at the sound of her voice. I turned back to Melinda. She was still standing there, at the end of the outer room, staring at me, with her strange half-smile. Silently I said goodbye to her, then raised my head to the light.

CHAPTER 16

"BABY!" MOM WHISPERED AS SHE HELPED ME OUT OF THE ground. Wrapping her arms around my shoulder, she walked me toward the house. "It's okay, honey, everything's all right now."

"Mom, the dolls—they got to Dad—" I babbled and then broke down crying. Nothing made any sense. All I knew was that Mom was here now and she would take care of me and everything would be okay. She'd find a way to make Dad into Dad and Melinda into Melinda, and we'd move and—

"It's okay," she said, "I'll explain everything." She opened the door to the house. I shook my head. *I don't want to go in there, you don't understand—*

"Inside, baby," she said. "It's all right now."

She sat me at the kitchen table. I was shaking. The room was empty. She brought back a blanket from the couch and wrapped it around my shoulders. Suddenly I was very tired. I wanted to close my eyes. All I could do was accept the blanket, and the tea my mother brought me, and sit with her.

"Mom," I said. "When d-did . . ."

"When did I get back?" she said. "Tonight. I came home early. Drink your tea."

I looked at her for the first time. She looked normal. No wooden features. She was my mom. I sipped my tea.

"Melinda is—"

"Yes, I know about Melinda. She's okay. She can't hurt you, baby. Trust me."

"Where's Dad?"

"He'll be down in a minute."

I croaked. "W-what's going on?"

Mom sipped. "Ooh, hot." She got up and dribbled some honey into the mug, blew on the surface of her drink. She stood with her back to the sink. "Honey," she said, "I'm tired. All the moving, the jobs. I can't sell homes forever. I just can't. I don't love it, you know? And you have to do what you love.

"Remember when you were a kid, and your dad would be off directing some big commercial, and we'd play dress-up and pretend we were walking the red carpet at the Oscars?"

I nodded.

"Your father and I had a plan, that one day, when he made a big movie, I would quit real estate and do something else. Something exciting. You know I was a model, back before you were born. I was gorgeous." Her eyes went soft and hazy. "The parties. The champagne. Once I had you, I lost my figure. It never came back.

"I'm not beautiful the way I used to be. Someone once told me I have what's called the 'Beauty Curse.' See, the problem with beauty is that it fades. Men are most valued in this society for their ideas. Women are most valued for their looks. I'm not happy about that, it's just a fact. Even celebrities who are slightly 'larger than normal,' as they say, well, you'll notice that they are still talked about in the media as being 'larger than normal.' There's always a story around our looks.

"Anyway, I'm rambling. I'm going to tell you everything, honey. Would you like that?"

I nodded.

Mom set her tea down. "Your father has the most important job of his life right now, and he's making the most important movie of this century."

The door to the kitchen opened gently. Dad walked in wearing a gentle smile, dressed casually in jeans and a T-shirt. He got a glass of water.

"I told you I was going to speak to her," Mom said, her volume rising.

I shrank in my chair. I couldn't look at him.

"This is all my fault," he said to Mom. "Let me tell her. I shouldn't have suggested we keep this from her when we moved."

"She wouldn't have understood," Mom said. They turned to each other, ignoring me.

"She would have when we found the doll. But she found it first, and by then you were out of town. I didn't feel right saying anything while you were away. I tried to keep it under wraps, but—" He turned to me. "I guess things don't always go as planned, eh, buckaroo?"

"What do you mean, before we moved?" I asked. "You knew about the dolls?"

Dad looked at me with tired eyes. "They're the reason we moved here, kiddo. To find them."

Mom put a hand on Dad's shoulder and turned to me. "Honey, the company hired your father to bring them this project. This older project. Because, technically, we own it."

"But Bill B. owns it! Or, he did," I blurted out before realizing it. I grew red.

"Honey," Mom said calmly, "we are his family. He was my grandfather. *Your* great-grandfather."

No. Couldn't be.

"But he was a *Nazi!*" The words sounded ridiculous, so melodramatic. My head was spinning. I felt dizzy.

Dad put his hand up as if to calm me. He called outside. "Melinda!"

The bell on the back door handle rang. Melinda entered, clutching the new doll to her chest. She smiled and walked to my mother, who put an arm around her. Like they were family. Suddenly I felt like an outsider.

"We're going to give you a choice," Dad said to me. "This is going to be the most famous family in America. In the world. Your mom and I made our decision already. She found her doll before she left. Now it's time for your decision."

"What decision?" I asked.

"To claim your birthright. To help finish the work of your great-grandfather. To change the world."

Mom sighed. "What do you want out of life, honey? Do you want to struggle? Struggle for money or to travel or through a job you hate? Do you really want to go through life avoiding people because you're ashamed of the way you look?"

I looked at the table. My whole body felt red-hot.

"I know what you go through, sweetie," Mom said. "I know how you feel. I've been there too. But now we can have it all. You'll never want for anything ever again. No bad looks from others, no feeling 'less than.' The doll will take care of that, forever. How would *that* make you feel?"

My jaw quivered. Soon something wet was dripping off my cheeks and into my lap. The pent-up emotions broke like a dam. The truth was, I didn't want any of these feelings anymore. Never feeling like I fit in. I always knew what others were saying. "She's fat. Look at her." I was tired of feeling embarrassed. My squirrel cheeks, always crimson. People could see right through me. That's why I preferred to be alone.

What would my life look like if I continued on this path? Would I be alone forever? A damsel, afraid to go outside and face the world?

Minutes passed. Mom gave me space; she understood, and I could see she understood, and I didn't have to say anything, and she helped me up and together we left the kitchen, the doll under her other arm.

"Take off your shoes, sweetie," she said softly, guiding me to the entryway where I could slide them off.

I looked up. She was lit from above by those horrible yellow lights. I was ready to give in to her, to go to sleep, to let the doll take me. For all this to be over.

And then I looked into her eyes.

They were not big and brown, like normal.

Her pupils seemed painted on. Her irises, a dull color. The veins in the white parts.

They were not her eyes.

And suddenly, I felt a surge of adrenaline that bolted me awake. Why was I contemplating this? Who was this woman in front of me?

"Come on, baby." Mom leaned in. Her eyes opened wider.

No.

No.

::shoves her mother as hard as she can::

I grabbed the doll, and the car keys on the little side table.

And I bolted.

CHAPTER 17

IT WASN'T UNTIL I'D RACED OUT OF THE DRIVEWAY, TIRES squealing, with the house in my rearview, that I realized no one was chasing me. No flailing arms, or hands with knives attached to them. Nothing. I thought it odd at the time, but only momentarily, and I gunned the car out of the neighborhood.

The doll was lying in the back seat, its stupid head bouncing with each hit of a pothole. I watched it in the rearview mirror. Unable to trust it to mind its own business, I snatched it up, screamed something incoherent, and flung it to the floor of the passenger side.

I figured I should move quickly, find a place to destroy it. Maybe Mom and Dad weren't chasing me because they knew it would be easier to call the cops and wait for them to pick me up. I wasn't sure. Best to keep going.

I drove up Franklin toward Hollywood, turned left on Western until I hit Wilshire. Took that toward West Hollywood, where rail-thin women like to walk rat-dogs and drink coffee.

As I passed a park on my right, a bright yellow light caught my attention. A flame. I looked closer. A trash can, on fire, with a bunch of people standing around it.

Yes. Wood. Fire.

I didn't let myself think.

I pulled over.

I MUST HAVE BEEN AN ODD SIGHT: A FAT SEVENTEEN-YEAR-old girl running toward this group of people, carrying a giant wooden doll. I know I looked batshit. I had dirt caked in my clothes and hair and I was soaked in sweat.

I held one hand up. Back away, I seemed to command. I've got to kill this thing.

I stared into the barrel. It seemed hot enough, but I needed to make sure. Grabbed more kindling from the pile next to the can and threw it in and fanned the flames until the fire roared and reached for the sky. If this godlike fire wasn't going to burn it up, I didn't know what would.

I heard a footstep behind me. A snap of a twig. I whipped around. A homeless woman stepped up next to me and stared into the fire.

I studied her face. She'd once been very pretty. Street life had taken its toll. Living outdoors does something to faces; exposure to the elements ages people. Her face was gaunt. I noticed her eyes the most, and not just because the flame-shadow was dancing off her pupils.

She stared into the fire, but not for warmth.

She looked at me, and I at her, and for a split second I saw myself. The fire seemed to dim, the air froze, and for that moment I glimpsed the true impact of what I was about to do.

Where will I go? I asked myself. What would I do without my family?

Suddenly, all this seemed ridiculous. I couldn't expect to burn this thing to a crisp and then just waltz back home. The truth was, I didn't see how I could return ever again. If I left them now, I left forever. Would I be a runaway? Emancipated? I had no money, no plan, and no clothes.

I looked again at the woman beside me. Was this my future? I waited for her to say something, but she didn't. She didn't have to.

The firelight reflected off the doll's head and caught

my eye. It looked quite a bit like me, actually, but skinnier. Of course, skinnier. An hourglass figure. Rosy cheeks and high cheekbones, painted on of course. A classic kind of beauty that never goes out of style.

Could it be my style, too?

I turned this over in my mind. To burn, or not to burn, that is the question. This would be a character in a huge movie. Which meant that if I let it take me, it could be *me* in a movie. It could be *me* with one million followers. It could be *me* on the big screen and on the posters lining Sunset and Hillhurst.

Wasn't that better than . . . this?

You're being ridiculous, I told myself. You can't do that. What about everything Dad told you?

No. Dad was joking, I thought. No studio would put Nazis in a movie. Don't be stupid.

The committee in my head raged on. I held the doll over the fire. The flames licked its feet.

But I didn't drop it. I could see myself in it, quite literally. My breasts on its narrow frame. My nose on its perfect face. It seemed to be combining all of my best features with its own, and suddenly some sap from a piece of a wood popped in the fire, and the fire belched and flung up yellow light, and I saw flash bulbs from cameras, a red carpet, and me with sparkling cheeks and a shimmery red dress. A boy on my arm. I glimpsed it in a flash, but it was more than enough, and when the flame receded, my cheeks were wet and salty again.

I thought about the school plays, the dancing alone in my room, the daydreams, the depression of looking at social media, feeling fat all the time, and—

I raised the doll over the fire for the last time. For a long time.

CHAPTER 18

I WALKED INTO THE HOUSE AND SET MY KEYS ON THE SIDE table. No one rushed up to greet me, nor to kill, cajole, or threaten me. I went to the kitchen and got a snack. I was starving. The sun had already risen. It was going to be a clear day with a blue sky.

I dropped the doll at my feet.

Dad entered, grabbed his bagel and coffee like it was any other day. He was late for work. So was Mom. They fluttered around, bumping into cabinets, straightening their clothes. Then there was Melinda. She was getting ready for school. I guess I had a sister now, from the looks of things.

Mom pecked me on the cheek and told me to stay home from school today and rest up. Melinda would get my assignments.

Then they were gone, and I was alone.

It always feels weird going to bed in the morning. The graveyard-shift lifestyle—I'm not cut out for it. I was so tired I could hardly think. I dragged myself upstairs, rinsed off in the shower, and collapsed into bed.

Closing my eyes, I prayed it would all be over by the time I woke up.

Chapter 19

It was, too. No half-doll jutting out of my shoulder. No wooden appendage for me to drag around all day. I noticed nothing, nothing at all.

I knew it was over right when I woke up, because I felt different. Normally I wake up with a thousand thoughts colliding like ancient armies, but this day I felt clear-headed.

If you were hoping for a triumphant story of good over evil, you may have to read something else. I'm not opposed to those stories—I like them, really I do—it's just not exactly *my* story.

The movie that was never supposed to be made is almost finished. After some finagling, Dad got Melinda and Mom and me on board as actresses. Yes, we are starring. Instead of an animation, the studio decided to make it into a live-action film. Heh heh. We've all signed on for a three-picture deal.

You'll soon see me in previews, on billboards all over the world. Me. My face. I won't tell you my real name or which movies I'll be in. But you might soon guess who I am. The message of Bill B. will live on in us. A new set of ideas will emerge in this country, then dominate it, and maybe the world too. You won't be able to stop them, no matter how hard you try. In fact, you'll feel drawn to them.

You'll see the films and then go to bed. And there, while you're sleeping, while your subconscious roams in some vast wilderness, our ideas will take root inside you and solidify. That's how it worked with the dolls, see? They integrated with us during deep sleep. And that's how it will work with all of you.

Some people will live. Most others will die. You'll either be killed—or converted into a killer. One of *our* killers.

Yes, we will rise. *You* will rise. The one true race will flourish once again.

May the Fourth Reich last 1,000 years.

Epilogue: Midnight

PUSHING AGAINST THE FLOOR WITH MY HAND, I SAT up. The stories, thunderous and profound, were over. Gathering the more than one hundred pages, I contemplated what I'd heard. Many possibilities, most of them contradictory. Which ones, if any, were really in our future?

The faceless being in front of me moved not an inch. To all appearances, it seemed dead.

I stood, stuffing my pages into my backpack and shouldering it.

I needed to find a way out.

I had two choices. One: I could revisit the hallway and try to find another room. But this didn't appeal to me. I figured the rooms only contained more stories.

There was a second option, which I knew intuitively.

I reached a hand toward the being and stepped

forward, my shoes squeaking on the linoleum floor.

My fingertips grazed its skin. It felt like cold gelatin.

The skin parted like water around my fingers, gently swallowing them. Then my hand. Then my wrist.

I wasn't scared; I knew the only way out was through. This was simply a gateway to . . . someplace else.

Up to my elbow now. The head was consuming me completely. My arm disappeared like it was part of a magic trick. The head gripped and sucked at me—and I let myself go all the way in, closing my eyes and holding my breath as I vanished altogether into the portal that was the thing's head.

AND I HAVE GLIMPSES. QUICK FLASHES OF MEMORIES. OF clinging onto the being's skull. Of it pulling me through the void of space. Then there was no void, no skull at all. Just a mellow darkness. That's all I remember.

I FELT THE THUMPS AND HEARD THE CHUG-CHUG-CHUG before opening my eyes. When I did, I saw a grey-carpeted world. I tried to blink it away. Turning to my right, the foggy, dew-covered terrain seemed to be rushing by me at great speed—grasslands and, beyond them, mountains. I was aboard a train, like the one I'd taken from California to Connecticut to find Pickering Cemetery.

I stood up from the couch. I was in a private car. A bed—my bed, I presumed—was made up nicely on a bunk at eye level. Opposite that were two pieces of luggage—mine.

How had I gotten here? Had I been transported through another portal? Or had Pickering Cemetery all been a dream?

Stepping out of my car, I peered down the narrow

corridor. A couple of people milled about. I walked down the hall and entered a dining car where passengers were drinking coffee and socializing. The clock on the wall read 9:03 a.m.

Things seemed normal. Two large screens on the wall opposite the tables played a commercial. Then text flashed on screen:

"SCAN YOUR CHILDREN. IT'S THE LAW."

I squinted. What law?

A voice interrupted my musings. "Mr. Schrader—"

I turned. A female attendant smiled. "We've extended your trip like you requested. You can stay in your car all the way to your destination."

Nonchalantly, I asked her what my destination was.

"New California," she said cheerfully before excusing herself to help another passenger.

New California?

Scratching my head, I turned back to the television. A newscast had begun.

"In a bizarre display, an unknown man showed up at the Federal Army Bureau in San Francisco today and began screaming. Standing at the bottom of the building . . ." An image of a soldier, head back, yelling, flashed on the screen.

Suddenly, my train bellowed. I lurched forward as it came to an abrupt halt.

Then—

A rumble. The train shook. Pictures on the walls, silverware on the tables, all vibrating.

An earthquake. I put a hand on the wall for support and waited for it to pass.

The speaker switched on. "Folks, we're going to be here a few minutes. Passing through earthquake country. We'll be rolling slowly into the station up ahead, should be stopped for thirty to sixty minutes. You're invited to stay on-board or get out and stretch your legs. The train station is earthquake-proof; there's no need to worry if you want to walk around the platform . . ."

A few minutes later, we stopped at the next station and I exited the train with a few other passengers. Earthquakes? I hadn't experienced any on my way to Connecticut.

Hot, damp air outside. The sky was grey; a dense fog had overtaken the station. It all had the feel of an impending nightmare.

I walked alongside the train. Everything *seemed* normal yet felt odd, as if I'd woken up from a long midday nap. Another earthquake struck—a small one this time.

A screen, mounted on a clear, plastic wall behind a station bench. News scrolled below a series of images. A male newscaster stared into the camera, unblinking. "Areas that suffered fallout from the nuclear blasts on the coast of the Pacific Northwest two weeks ago have been deemed 'Safe' by government officials . . ."

I stepped closer. The screen showed an overhead view of the coast off "New California." A seaside town had been reduced to rubble. Broken cliffs fell into the sea. It looked like a magnificent claw had swiped up a portion of land before flinging it across the sky.

There was no nuclear blast before I left home, I thought. My head began to spin as I recounted the oddities I'd seen in the last thirty minutes: New California, nuclear blasts, families being "scanned," a screaming man . . .

Oh, no.

I turned and froze when I saw it.

The digital billboard about fifty yards down the track,

standing high above the platform.

The young girl, a face of Hollywood beauty, stared down at me.

And to the right of her face, the title:

SEE YOU IN THEATRES

Coming soon, the text beneath it read.

Suddenly, I knew. I hadn't been taken back to my world. This was some alternate one, an amalgamation of the stories I'd received from the room within the walls.

What was I to do now?

And how would I get home?

TO BE CONTINUED . . .

ZΦΦ

Bonus Short Film for Readers Only!*

Tour the Los Angeles zoo as we chronicle the animals' upcoming escape attempt—and the zookeeper's efforts to stop them. (9 mins)

Watch now exclusively at:
https://www.andrewjschrader.com/zoo

Directed by Andrew Schrader
Soundtrack by Thee Oh Sees

*ZΦΦ exclusive to readers until December 31, 2019.

Acknowledgements

Thanks to Jordan Harris for the cover design and help on "See You In Theatres," Rickey Mizuno for the cover photography, Blake Sheldon for his modeling skills, and Abby Cooper, Travis Schirmer, and Michael Brittain for their notes. Also, Karen Conlin for her editing (she's the best, you should hire her). Of course, thanks to ye readers.

"Croakman" was inspired by the film *The Look of Silence.*

About the Author

Andrew Schrader is a Los Angeles-based writer and director known for his unconventional storytelling and stark visual style. He's the co-director of two feature films, including *The Age of Reason*.

He's written for tech companies in San Francisco and Silicon Valley, and his music videos for bands Oh Sees and White Reaper have been featured in Paste Magazine and Stereogum. He's the author of three books, including *What Goes On in the Walls at Night*, which was featured on the Reddit No Sleep podcast and awarded Best Fantasy Book of 2018 by Red City Review.

Please support this book by:

1. Signing up for the mailing list at www.andrewjschrader.com

2. Leaving a review on Amazon and Goodreads

3. Sharing a purchase link with your friends or family

4. Following on Facebook at www.facebook.com/andrewjschrader

46794403R00130

Made in the USA
Middletown, DE
01 June 2019